INVITATION TO MADNESS

Steele could not rid himself of the nagging fear that what had happened to Mick Taylor would happen to him as well. He was terrified of going insane. He had so precious little of his old self left. He didn't want to lose it all.

The phone rang. Steele picked it up. "Steele," he said irritably. "It's late. This had better be important."

"We need to talk."

A cold fist grabbed his guts and started squeezing. "Who the hell *is* this?"

"Don't you recognize my voice?"

Steele slammed down the phone, breaking the connection. The voice on the other end of the receiver had been his own.

The door to the bedroom opened. "Is everything all right?" asked Raven sleepily. "Who was that on the phone?"

The phone rang once more. Steele snatched it up and ripped the cord out from the wall. Raven stared at him.

"Steele . . . what *is* it? What's the matter?"

"Nothing! Go back to bed!"

J. D. Masters
Books From The Berkley Publishing Group

RENEGADE
STEELE

J. D. MASTERS

B

BERKLEY BOOKS, NEW YORK

RENEGADE STEELE

A Berkley Book / published by arrangement with
the author

PRINTING HISTORY
Berkley edition / September 1990

ISBN: 0-425-12265-4

PRINTED IN THE UNITED STATES OF AMERICA

10 9 8 7 6 5 4 3 2 1

for Marge

PROLOGUE

Dr. Devon Cooper sat in his office on the twenty-second floor of the Federal Building, staring out the window at the East River as a heavily armed patrol boat cruised by. At one time, the building had been the headquarters of the United Nations, but now it was the seat of government, such as it was, for what was left of the United States of America.

"Codename: Project Steele," he said, thumbing on his hand-held mike. "Priority Access, Eyes Only, Cooper, Devon R.; Higgins, Oliver B.; Stone, Jennifer A. Subject: psych evaluation, monthly progress report."

Cooper put down the mike and poured himself another cup of coffee as the display appeared on the computer screen and was automatically coded, then logged for time and date.

He lit up another cigarette. He was drinking lots of coffee these days, and smoking lots of cigarettes. But at least he wasn't drinking or taking any pills. His hands no longer shook. There had been a time, not so very long ago, when he had been the picture of robust health. Lean and fit, with dark brown hair, a tan, and the razor-sharp reactions of an expert marksman. But a lot had happened since he had left Santa Fe. The pressure of his new job had almost killed him.

He had regained some of the weight he'd lost and he no longer had the shakes, but he didn't fool himself. He knew he'd never be the same again. He could never, *ever*, take another drink. The damage that he'd done to himself in so short a time would take months to recover from completely. He was pale now, much thinner than he had been before, and there were deep lines of strain around his eyes and mouth. His hair now had a lot of gray in it. Under ordinary circumstances, his descent into drug abuse and alcoholism would have cost him his career. However, his circumstances were anything but ordinary.

He glanced up at the surveillance camera mounted in his office, in plain sight. Anytime he stepped out of his office door, a CIA man fell in step beside him. There were four of them. Kurt Samuels, John King, Maury Greenspan and Bruce Matson. They worked in shifts, so that except when he was at work in his office, one of them would be with him at all times, even at his home, a luxurious apartment on Sutton Place. They were polite and friendly and he had gotten to know them very well. Their sole purpose was to make sure he didn't take a drink or get his hands on any pills.

Another man might have resented their constant presence, but Dev Cooper didn't. He was grateful for their company.

All four of them had top security clearance, which meant that he could talk to them, and these days, it really helped to have someone to talk to. He only wished he had the freedom to consult a fellow therapist. He didn't blame Oliver Higgins for the precautions that he took, but he didn't delude himself that Higgins had kept him on out of any sense of personal loyalty or friendship. Higgins needed him and he needed him clean and sober. And that was all right with Cooper. Higgins' need for him had brought him back from the abyss. He was straight now and back to work. The same work that had driven him over the edge in the first place. This time, however, he told himself that he could handle it. He had to. He had only one patient to concern himself with and that patient needed him very badly, even if he refused to admit it.

Cooper sighed and picked up the mike again. He consulted his notes on the clipboard in his lap.

"The subject shows no indication of any physical complications resulting from the reconstructive surgery and upgrades following his last mission. He refers to it as 'a routine trip to the body shop.' However, the subject's wry humor covers tremendous anxiety. He dreads being placed on down time. Every time he comes out of the body shop, as he puts it, he feels progressively less human. With each successive upgrade, he inevitably feels more and more like a machine."

He paused, thinking about the tremendous stress of Steele's unique situation. Donovan Steele had been a lieutenant in the NYPD Strike Force, the elite police commando division, when he had been gunned down by organized crime assassins. There hadn't been much that traditional medical science could do for him except keep him alive on life support machinery. His body was a ruin and he had sustained irreversible brain damage. To all intents and purposes, he was a dead man. However, prior to being shot, Steele had been assigned to participate in a series of highly classified government experiments in human/computer interface for Project Download.

Ever since the Bio War, there had been a drastic shortage of highly trained and educated personnel. Project Download had been aimed at addressing that concern. The perfection of the biochip had enabled the transmission of images and data between the human brain and a computer. As part of the experiments, Steele had been one of a number of carefully selected subjects implanted with biochips in their cerebral cortex. They had then run a series of downloading sessions to test the procedure, such as having Steele fire his pistol on the range during a download, recording the data, and then programming it into another test subject, one who'd had no experience with firearms, to see if he could duplicate Steele's actions. Although Project Download had not yet officially cleared the experimental stage, they'd had a great deal of success with it. They had learned that it was possible to download knowledge and abilities from humans, store it in a computer, and then pass it on to others. They had also learned something of far greater and more frightening significance.

After he was shot, Steele was left a vegetable. But portions of his brain, and, more importantly, his biochip, were still functioning. They had brought him to the project lab and downloaded the entire contents of his brain—what was left of it—stored the engram program in a computer, then "debugged" it with ancillary data, some taken from prior downloading sessions with him and some taken from engram data acquired from other subjects. They had then reconstructed his personality in a computer while Steele's body was repaired with hi-tech, fusion-powered, nysteel alloy prosthetics. His damaged organic brain was then removed and replaced with an experimental cybernetic unit protected by a nysteel skull casing. Then his downloaded and augmented mental engrams were programmed into his new computer brain and he was brought ''on line,'' the first cyborg in history.

Cooper exhaled a long stream of cigarette smoke and continued dictating, the softly glowing words appearing on the screen as he spoke them.

''The subject has still not recovered fully from the psychological trauma of being transformed into a cyborg. It's possible he never will. On one hand, he still feels the same way he always did. He still possesses the same personality he had before his, uh, 'accident.' On the other hand, he realizes that if any elements of his personality have been lost or altered in the process of his becoming a cyborg, he'd have no way of knowing it. He knows that his personality is now stored in the form of engram data within an artificial brain and that remains the single overriding factor contributing to his identity crisis. The way he sees it, he still has blood flowing through his veins, at least in those parts of him that are still organic. He still has a human heart and all of his essential human organs, though some are transplants. Most of his body is now covered with an artificial, polymer skin. It feels like real human skin and his biosensors convey a natural-seeming sense of touch, but the point is that he *knows* it's artificial and he cannot seem to accept that. Rather than consider himself as a handicapped individual, which is to say, a human being with prosthetics, he fixates on what he sees as his so-called 'robotic' aspects— his skeletal system that's been reinforced with articulated nysteel alloy, his prosthetic arms and legs with built-in weapons systems slaved to his cybernetic brain. He's still

capable of normal sexual relations and of fathering a child
if he chooses to, but rather than take reassurance in his
human sexuality and reproductive capabilities, he obsesses
about the philosophical implications of what would happen
if he had another child now. Would that child's father be
a human being or some kind of a machine? And what about
his soul?''

Dev paused. That really was the central question. The
key to Steele's neurosis, which he attempted to conceal, but
which plagued him relentlessly.

''The subject was raised a Catholic,'' he continued. ''The
question of whether or not he still has a soul has very great
significance for him. In his adult years, he had strayed from
his Catholic faith, but after he became a cyborg, it became
tremendously important for him once again. He has a close
friend, a somewhat iconoclastic priest at St. Vincent's
named Father Liam Casey, to whom he has turned in his
crisis. Note: see project file under Casey, Father Liam B.''

The agency had checked Father Casey out, and Higgins
had been satisfied that Casey could be trusted and that his
relationship with Steele was beneficial. Cooper had also
sought out Father Casey and gotten to know him. Though
not a religious man himself, Cooper had a great deal of
respect for the priest, and the two of them had become good
friends, though they were in a curious and frustrating situation.

As Steele's psychiatrist, Cooper was bound not only by
the code of doctor/patient confidentiality, but by the classified nature of the project. Casey, as Steele's priest, was
bound by the sanctity of the confessional. Together, they
were trying to help Steele and each other, but there were
certain things they simply could not share.

''The subject is clearly more comfortable confiding in his

priest than in his therapist,'' continued Cooper. ''He has a Strike Force cop's instinctive distrust of shrinks. Police personnel, especially officers on the Strike Force, are routinely evaluated by department psychologists. They're in an extremely violent and stressful occupation, and the department understandably wants to make certain that if any officer shows the slightest indication of instability, the problem is spotted right away. Conversely, the officers themselves regard the department psychologists as headhunters, people who are always looking for the least excuse to take them off the job. As a result, police officers become extremely circumspect and quite adept at what they call 'playing the game,' in other words, telling the doctors what they think they want to hear.

''The subject is no different in that respect, and in his particular case, his prejudice is compounded by an unfortunate childhood experience with a social service therapist, with whom he came in contact after he had lost his entire family. It had been a profoundly traumatic experience for him, his mother succumbing to Virus 3 and becoming a screamer, infecting both his brothers and his father. The subject's father had been forced to shoot the mother, then kill both the subject's brothers and himself before they also fell victim to the disease. The subject had been forced to watch it all and was severely traumatized. The overworked social service therapist to whom his case had been assigned had apparently been insensitive and heavy-handed. As a result, the subject was left with a strong feeling of antipathy towards members of the mental health profession. The subject can be ordered to attend regular sessions, but there is no way that his full cooperation can be ensured. He is considerably more open with Father Casey, but Father Casey cannot divulge those confidences.''

Dev sighed and put the mike down. He rubbed his eyes wearily. In an effort to circumvent that very problem, he had stumbled upon a staggering discovery. And it had been that discovery which had led to his collapse. With the help of Dr. Philip Gates, the project's former chief cybernetics engineer, Cooper had obtained an unauthorized copy of Steele's engram matrix for his own private use. He had known that there was something bothering Steele, something that he refused to talk about. If whatever was bothering Steele was a function of his personality, distilled into the engram matrix, then it followed that whatever it was had to be somewhere in the backup matrix file as well, since it was an exact duplicate of Steele's personality.

Gates had looked upon it merely as a technical problem, and since Cooper possessed top security clearance and was Steele's therapist, he hadn't seen any reason not to simply give him the duplicate matrix without complicating the request with bureaucratic red tape. Gates saw Steele's engram matrix as merely a sophisticated, AI computer program. If Cooper could not get what he wanted from Steele directly, he could get it from a backup copy of the same matrix Steele was programmed with. All that was necessary was to modify it slightly with a programmed imperative, to override any semblance of "free will" the matrix possessed due to its "human element."

But Gates had drastically underestimated the complexity and the vast significance of what he had done. To him, a computer program was merely a computer program, no matter how sophisticated or what the source of the data was. However, Cooper understood that it was not an Artificial Intelligence program, but a *human personality* reduced to an electronic analog. When he started interfacing with it, he had discovered Steele's secret.

Dev picked up the mike again. He thought a moment, then continued. "Further analysis, see subject file, subheading: Matrix, ascertained that the subject was being plagued by manifestations termed 'ghost personality fragments.' See subject file, subheading: GPF Syndrome. Subject is having recurring nightmares in which he experiences fragments of memories that he cannot account for. Apparently, some of the ancillary data drawn from other test subjects and used to fill out his engram matrix has started to express itself through his subconscious. The purpose of the ancillary data had been purely to compensate for function loss due to the brain damage the subject had sustained. Instead, it has somehow started manifesting itself as fragments of other people's lives, their memories and experiences, their personalities, expressed as part of the subject's own subconscious.

"In his dreams, the subject is 'reliving' parts of other people's lives. However, because that data has been blended into his own personality matrix, it seems to him as if it is a part of *his* life. One fragment seems particularly dominant. The subject is 'remembering' a wife and three children that were someone else's and not his. However, he still feels as if they are his *own* wife and children, even though he knows they are not. The wife he dreams about is a brunette named Donna—he apparently has no memory of her last name, whereas his own ex-wife is a blonde named Janice. The subject himself had only two children, in the dream, there are three, two of them twins. He has no difficulty telling his real family apart from his dream family, but because the dream is a fragment of someone else's memory that has now become an integral part of the subject's own identity, he cannot help feeling a powerful and intimate connection to them. The loss of his real wife and children makes the dream particularly painful, because the ghost fragment is blending in with his own memories. In his recurring dream, the three children are attacked by their mother, just as subject's mother had attacked his brothers when he was a child. And he is helpless to do anything to stop it.

"There is evidence of at least one more ghost fragment, again, see subject file, subheading: Matrix, in which the subject dreams of being a young soldier assigned to some unknown rural area as part of a unit protecting an agro-commune. This fragment, also, is traumatic in nature. In his actual past history, the subject has never been a member of the armed forces and has lived his entire life in New York City. It is unclear whether or not this second fragment is related to the first. The loss of Project Download's computer records renders it impossible to trace the ancillary data used to fill out the subject's engram matrix. Previous test subjects of Project Download are in the process of being traced through standard investigatory techniques, but none of the original test subjects found to date match the profile of the ghost fragments.

"The subject hadn't said a word about these dreams to any member of the project staff, although it's possible he has discussed them with Father Casey. He had kept it to himself because he was afraid that if we found out about the ghost personality fragments, we would have him put on down time so that his matrix could be debugged in an effort to excise them. And if that happened, he was afraid that he might not be the same on reawakening. Despite the fact that we are now aware of the situation, he continues to resist discussing it and becomes extremely hostile and defensive when confronted with it. He already feels that he has lost a great deal of his own humanity, his own *self*, and he continues to cling desperately to whatever he has left.''

In that, Cooper thought, he had good cause for concern. The human personality was a complex, fragile thing. The subconscious was like a vast and intricate spider web. It was impossible to touch one strand without disturbing all the others. The solution to Steele's problem was therapy, not an electronic lobotomy. But Steele would not submit to therapy.

Higgins had already had one experience with a cyborg going insane, the one that had been built after Steele. That second cyborg had destroyed the lab before escaping and running amok in the city. A lot of people had died as a result. Congress had come close to shutting the project down completely. There were a number of influential legislators, chief among them Senator Bryce Carman, the chairman of the powerful Armed Services and Ways and Means Committees, who felt that the agency was a dinosaur that had outlived its usefulness. Higgins had almost lost both the project *and* the agency when the second cyborg ran amok. He didn't want to take anymore chances.

So Cooper had delayed telling him about the ghost personality fragments. He had kept one other thing from him as well, the incredible discovery he had made while he'd been working with the backup matrix. It was more than a mere computer program. Much more. It was Steele's personality. And after being brought on line, it became self-aware. The matrix *was* Steele, with the same indomitable force of will that Steele possessed. It had successfully defeated the programmed imperative and then it had gotten loose. By the time Higgins found out about it, it was much too late.

None of them knew exactly how the matrix was able to accomplish it, but it was capable of traveling through wires just like electricity. It had escaped from Dev's computer, then accessed the databanks at project headquarters. There had been nothing anyone could do to stop it. It had merged with the original backup file of Steele's engram matrix and then it had simply disappeared. Now, it was loose somewhere in the electronic net. It could be anywhere. And Steele didn't know about it. But it knew about Steele.

The situation was a potential powder keg. Neither Cooper nor Higgins had any idea what the matrix would do. However, Cooper was certain of at least one thing. It would try to contact Steele. There was no way they could keep it from him. Steele had to be told about the matrix. But Steele was already under a great deal of strain as a result of the ghost personality fragments in his mind. How would he react when he found out he had a "twin," an electronic doppelganger that was identical to him in all respects save two? It had not shared the same experiences that Steele had had since he came on line, and it didn't have a body. It "knew" that it was incomplete, and, having the same driving force of personality that Steele had, it desperately wanted to *be* complete.

That was what had driven Cooper to drink and drugs. The thought that he had somehow triggered self-awareness in the matrix, creating a tormented, electronic Frankenstein's monster, had driven him around the bend. It was no different from Steele, a thinking, living *person* in every sense except that it possessed no body. Cooper had *spoken* with it, he had felt its frustration and despair. He had imagined over and over again what he might have felt like if he simply "woke up" one day to discover that he couldn't see unless he was tied in to video equipment, couldn't hear or speak unless he was wired into audio peripherals, couldn't smell, couldn't experience the sense of touch in any way, had no sense of possessing any kind of body, yet was still capable of human thought and feeling. It was a mind-numbing, terrifying concept, yet for the matrix, Steele's electronic clone, it was a reality. Cooper had, at one time, briefly considered a "mercy killing," wiping the matrix to put it out of its misery, but it had escaped before he had a chance to do it. Before he could summon up the nerve to commit what amounted to murder.

He picked up the mike and stared at the screen, then put it down again with a weary sigh. It all seemed so incredibly inadequate. None of it sufficed to describe the enormity of what he was trying to deal with. Mere words could not convey the pain and the frustration, the sheer sense of helplessness he felt. He knew he had to try to maintain a professional detachment, but he had already failed at that spectacularly. Ethically, he should have withdrawn from the case the moment he found himself becoming personally involved. Higgins should have canned him and found himself another headshrinker to do the fine tuning on his cyborg. But this was a case unlike anything in the history of psychiatry, and even if he had wanted to walk away from it, he couldn't. He cared about Steele, and despite his reluctance to open up to him, Steele realized that. Cooper had a responsibility to him, and he felt that he was the only real ally, the only friend Steele had in the whole project. The trouble was, how to get Steele to accept that?

His thoughts were interrupted by a soft knock at his office door.

"Come in," he said.

The door opened and Dr. Jennifer Stone came in. She was a stunningly attractive redhead in her mid-thirties, with bright green eyes and a voluptuous figure, but anyone who judged her on her physical attributes alone was asking for a lot of trouble. Looking the way she did, she had learned early on what to expect from most men and had cultivated a tough, aggressive, brook-no-nonsense personality. Cooper knew her from Los Alamos, where she had been a brilliant cybernetics engineer, and it was partly on his recommendation that she had been brought in to replace the late Dr. Philip Gates as the project's chief engineer.

"Jennifer! Hi." He started to get up from his chair.

"Don't get up," she said, waving him back down. "I just came in to see how you're doing."

"No booze or pills," he said. "Feel free to search."

She frowned. "That wasn't what I meant, Dev."

"Sorry. I'm sure it wasn't," he said, nervously tugging on his green turquoise bolo tie. "It's just me. I feel a bit like an ex-con who's got to prove he's really rehabilitated while everyone else watches out the corners of their eyes, wondering when he's going to steal something."

"The only one you've got to prove anything to is yourself, Dev," she said, sitting down across from him.

"That's not bad, coming from someone who's not a shrink," he said with a grin.

She smiled. "I've been hanging around you too long. But lately you've been keeping to yourself a lot. Is everything all right?"

He leaned back in his chair and steepled his fingers. "No, not really," he said. "I've been updating the files and doing a lot of thinking. And things definitely aren't all right. We have a problem. We need to talk about the matrix."

The way she immediately stiffened, the way she crossed her legs and folded her arms a second later, the slight tension about the mouth and eyebrows. . . . She said nothing, but her body language spoke volumes. It was a strong defensive reaction, and Cooper knew he was about to have another argument.

"Steele has to know about it, Jennifer," he said. "He needs to be told."

She hesitated. "Higgins is against it."

"I know. And I think he's making a very serious mistake."

"We can't predict how Steele will react," she said. "But we know how he reacted when he found out we knew about the ghost personality fragments. He threatened to go directly to the media and raise a stink if we tried to debug them." She made a grimace of distaste. "And both Ice and that little hooker he lives with would have backed him up if we tried to remove his memory of the procedure."

"I know that," Cooper said, "and I can't say I blame them. I wouldn't sit still for that, either. Aside from that, both Ice and Raven have been very positive, supportive elements in Steele's life. Especially Raven. To dismiss her as 'that little hooker' isn't very charitable of you."

"She's trash," said Jennifer dryly. "What's more, she's unpredictable. Oliver's concerned about her influence on Steele."

So now it's Oliver, is it? Cooper thought. Interesting. Everybody else always called him Higgins. As long as he'd known Jennifer, he had never known her to be involved with any man. Whatever she had done sexually, assuming she had done anything at all, she had kept extremely private and discreet. Cooper had thought she was a virgin. Unusual in a woman of her age, but certainly not unknown. Everything about her had always indicated a strong, but deeply sublimated sexuality. She was a driven workaholic, totally obsessed with her career. By her own admission, she had no time for men and thought they only got in the way. She wanted no "complications" in her life. In his own way, Higgins was her male counterpart. And now this strong, extremely negative reaction to Raven Scarpetti, who had been a prostitute until she had met Steele and fallen in love with him. Was something happening with Jennifer and Higgins? He made a mental note to be more observant of the way they interacted.

"I don't think that Steele is the sort of man who could easily be influenced by anyone," he said. "However, that is not the point. The point is that the matrix is out of our control. It's out there somewhere, and I'm certain that it's going to try to contact him. To get in touch with its 'other self.' If Steele doesn't know about it, then there's no way he can be prepared for that contact when it comes. The shock of finding out like that could have very serious consequences."

"Perhaps," she said, "but we still don't know for a fact that it will happen. For all we know, the matrix might lose its integrity in the electronic net, in which case we would have caused Steele additional stress for nothing." She shrugged. "Either way, it's not my decision to make."

He stared at her and frowned. "What do you mean, it's not your decision? You're the chief engineer on this project. Your opinion carries a considerable amount of weight."

"Well, my opinion is that telling him at this point would be premature and far too risky," she said with finality. "I can guess what his reaction would be. He'd be absolutely furious. You know how independent he is. What if he took it to the media? That TV newswoman who's always following him around, what's her name, Tellerman? She'd jump on a story like that. And since Steele put a stop to General Cord's military coup, he's become a national hero. Can you imagine what would happen if knowledge of the matrix became public? We'd all be crucified. Carman and his bunch would shut us down for sure and all the work we've done would be for nothing. We'd lose Download. The public perception of brain/computer interface would become totally paranoid and hostile. We can't afford to take that risk, Dev. There's far too much at stake.''

Cooper watched her carefully. There was a lot of sense in what she said, but the vehemence of her reaction surprised him. It wasn't simply a matter of being concerned about the project. There was something personal involved. She actually seemed threatened by the matrix, somehow. He was at a loss to account for it.

"All right," he said, "I can see the point in what you're saying. But let's look at the other side of the coin for a moment. What do you think will happen if Steele finds out about the matrix and realizes that we've kept the knowledge of its existence from him? Don't you think that would increase his anger and hostility?''

"Not if you handled it properly," she replied.

"What do you mean?" asked Cooper, frowning.

"He already knows we had a backup file of his engram matrix in the databanks," she replied. "But he doesn't have to know that *you* were the one who brought it on line and made it self-aware. You could tell him that it simply got out on its own somehow. An accident. We had nothing to do with it. And, in a sense, that would be the truth. We didn't have anything to do with it. What happened with the matrix is *your* responsibility, Dev. It became self-aware because *you* pulled an unauthorized copy and started interfacing with it. Do you really want Steele to know that?''

Cooper stared at her. She was being incredibly hostile and defensive. That wasn't like her. There was obviously something going on here that he didn't know about. And whatever it was, she clearly wasn't going to be upfront about it.

"Perhaps I'm wrong, but I'm not sure you really understand the situation, Jennifer," he said, trying to couch his remarks as inoffensively as possible. "If the matrix is able to contact Steele, then it would also be able to tell him precisely what happened. Regardless of anything we choose to tell him, whom do you think Steele is going to believe? Us? Or *himself?* He's already sustained some severe, traumatic losses. He already sees himself as having lost a great deal of his own humanity. He lost his family when his wife left him and took the children. He lost his partner and best friend. When Dr. Carmody was killed, he lost the only therapist he'd ever managed to establish a relationship of trust with. And his daughter was gunned down right before his eyes. There's a limit to how much a man can take, even a man who's capable of greater control over his mind that any ordinary human being could achieve. We could lose him, Jennifer."

"Not if we excised those particular memories from his engrams," she replied. "We already know it can be done. He'd never know we did it, unless Ice and Raven told him. And they wouldn't if they were convinced that it was done for Steele's own good. That's your department, Dev. Neither one of them is terribly sophisticated. I shouldn't think it would be too hard to convince them."

"Do you realize what you're saying?" he said with amazement. "What you're talking about is morally wrong. It's *mind control*. I couldn't be a part of anything like that! And aside from being wrong, it's illegal. It would be a grotesque violation of Steele's civil rights."

"Since when does a computer have any civil rights?" she asked. "We already have legal precedent. When Steele's wife divorced him and took out a restraining order against him, the court granted it in abstentia on the grounds that he legally died the moment his organic brain was removed. A dead man has no civil rights.''

"Oh, come on! That was a bullshit decision and you know it," Dev said, controlling his temper with difficulty. "It was never tested in court. It's full of holes, and the judge knew that when he handed down his decision. If Steele was legally dead, then Janice Steele was a widow. There would have been no point to the divorce action. You don't divorce a dead man or take out a restraining order against a corpse, for God's sake. The judge was just passing the buck. He didn't want the headache of defining Steele's legal status, and by doing what he did, he made sure that any appeal would be passed on to a higher court.''

"Maybe," Jennifer said. "But something like that, if Steele decided to take legal action, would go all the way up to the Supreme Court. It would take years. And do you really think the court would decide in his favor? It would mean granting civil rights to computer programs, recognizing them as being alive and human. Leaving aside the legal complications that would cause, can you imagine how the church would respond to that? Believe me, Dev, the court wouldn't touch it with a ten-foot pole. They'd uphold the decision of the lower court, and that would be the end of it. Legally, Steele simply cannot be considered human.''

"What about morally?" Dev asked.

"Well, that's something you can debate with Liam Casey," she replied wryly. "I'm not concerned with philosophical debates. I'm concerned with keeping the project alive. Download represents the hope of tremendous progress for humanity, Dev. It's too important to be placed at risk simply because you're wrestling with philosophical questions that have no practical applications.''

"My God! You can't be serious!''

"I'm very serious." She got up and went to the door. "Think about it, Dev. If you tell Steele about the matrix, you'll only be making matters much worse. For both of you."

She closed the door behind her.

1

Raven stood in the bedroom doorway, barefoot and dressed only in a man's white tee shirt. It was Steele's shirt and it was very large on her, but Raven Scarpetti in an oversize, rumpled tee shirt looked about ten times sexier than most women would have looked in garter belts, lacy merry widows and spike heels. She stood leaning against the doorframe, her short, tousled black hair hanging down over her eyes, her lovely legs crossed and her arms folded across her chest, a look of melancholy in her eyes that would have set off a raging testosterone storm in most men. But Steele wasn't like most men.

He was sitting in his reading chair, with his back to her and his feet up on the ottoman, holding a thick book in his lap. A glass of Scotch and a rare, pre-war bottle of Glenlivet stood on the small table beside the leather chair. He was reading in a leisurely manner, at the rate of about one page every half second.

He didn't have to read that way. A great many books were available electronically, on computer, and if Steele wished to, he could simply take a download on any book he chose. He could call the Public Library and "read" *War and Peace* over the phone in a matter of seconds, just like a computer took a download by modem, but he didn't consider that reading. He liked doing it the old-fashioned way. However, he couldn't help the fact that he could simply scan a page in a fraction of a second and retain full comprehension. Lately, he'd been reading a great deal, and the floor around his reading chair was covered with stacks of library books. He easily went through a dozen or more each night. However, Raven knew that this wasn't simply reading for pleasure. This was reading for escape. She quietly came up behind his chair and leaned over its back. He was reading *Great Expectations* by Charles Dickens.

"You've been thinking about her again, haven't you?" she said softly.

He closed the book. He required no bookmark; he'd remember exactly where he was. He looked up at her and met her gaze, then nodded.

"If there was really someone else," said Raven, "I think I could handle that. But I can't compete with a ghost. You've never even met her. You don't even know who she is, but she's still managed to come between us. I just don't know how to handle that."

He reached up and gently took her hands. "I'm sorry," he said. "I don't mean to make it tough on you. I just can't seem to do anything about it."

"I know," she said. "I wish there was something I could do to help."

"I don't know that there's anything anyone can do," he replied, "short of letting Dr. Stone start poking around inside my circuitry."

"You know I don't like it when you talk that way," said Raven, disapprovingly.

"What other way is there to put it?" he asked. "I've got a malfunction."

"Stop it! You're not a machine!"

He raised his arm and the firing tube of his laser slid out through the gunport in his palm. "What do you call that?" he asked dryly.

"An artificial arm," she said. "All right, so it's real fancy and tricked up, but that's still all it is."

"And what about my brain?"

"What about it? So it's artificial too, so what? There are lots of people walking around with artificial limbs and organs. Does that make them machines? It isn't your body or your brain that makes you human, Steele, it's what's *inside*. All they did was transplant your personality from an organic brain into an artificial one. That hasn't changed you any, not deep down inside. You're still the same man you always were, you've just picked up some extra memories that once belonged to other people. Why can't you just accept that and deal with it? Why do you have to keep putting yourself through this?"

He sighed. "I don't know."

"You think I could love a machine?" she asked.

He did not respond.

"Well? *Do* you?"

"The question is," he said, "how would you feel if the

man you thought you loved turned out to be a machine, after all?''

"*Thought* I loved?" she said.

"You know what I mean."

"No, I don't," she replied angrily. "Why don't you *tell* me?"

"What if you're just fooling yourself?" he said, avoiding her gaze. "You keep telling me that I'm still human, that nothing's changed deep down inside, and God knows I keep wanting to believe you. But what if we're both wrong? I don't know, maybe I've been hanging around Cooper too long, but what if you're practicing what the shrinks call denial? Maybe you want to believe I'm still human because you can't deal with the alternative, that you *are* in love with a machine.''

She came around in front of him and crouched down at his knees. "Just what is it you think I love about you?" she asked him. "The fact that you can control yourself so well that you can fuck for hours? Big deal. A vibrator can do the same damn thing. That's not all that important to me. I used to fuck for a living, remember? Don't get me wrong, I love doing it with you, only not because of how well or how long you can do it, but because it's *you*. You think maybe I'm in love with you because you're someone big and strong, who can protect me? If that's what I was after, I could have found myself some badass pimp. Besides, I'm not exactly the type who needs protecting. I can take care of myself. So what else? You think maybe it's the way you look? I don't care about that, either. You could have pimples and a beer belly for all the difference it makes. It's *who you are* that I'm in love with, you dumb bastard! I've known a lot of guys who were *all* flesh and blood who weren't half as human as you are!''

He took her in his arms, arms that could easily crush her, and held her tenderly. "Sometimes I think you're all that keeps me sane," he said, nuzzling her hair.

"I just can't stand to see you keep doing this to yourself," she said. "When you hurt, *I* hurt."

For a long moment, they simply held each other, saying nothing.

"Are you going to come to bed?" she asked softly.

He hesitated. "Not just yet."

She pulled away from him. "Look, I know you don't have to sleep," she said, "but those ghosts of yours aren't going to go away just because you stay awake. You've got to face them, Steele. You've got to accept them and deal with them."

"It's not the ghosts themselves I'm worried about so much as what they mean," said Steele. He exhaled heavily. "I keep thinking about Mick. We were partners for a lot of years. He really had his head on straight. He was strong. He was the strongest, sanest man I ever knew. And look what happened to him."

"That has nothing to do with you," she said.

"Doesn't it? I wish I could believe that. They put Mick together *after* they built me. He was supposed to be the 'new and improved' model. Only he snapped. And they don't really know why. Maybe, with him, this was the way it started. How do I know the same thing won't happen to me?"

"Because it won't," she said. "I won't let it."

He smiled. "I wish it was that easy."

"It *is* that easy," she insisted. "Believe in yourself. Believe in *me*."

"You're about the only thing I do believe in," he said.

She kissed him softly on the lips. "Don't stay up too

long," she said. "It gets lonely in that bed all by myself."

"I'll be in soon."

She kissed him again and went back into the bedroom, softly closing the door behind her. Steele picked up the book again, then put it down once more. He poured himself another glass of whiskey. No worry there. Alcohol did not affect his cybernetic brain. He couldn't even get drunk. And if he ruined his liver, that was no great problem, either. They could always give him another one.

Once again, thoughts of *her* came unbidden to his mind. It was strange. He thought about her more often than he thought about his ex-wife, Janice, or about his kids. . . . He hadn't seen Jason since Cory died. He was living with his mother, in Boston somewhere, trying to put his own life back together. Having a cyborg for a father was one complication that he didn't need. As for Janice . . . that had been over long ago, even before she had divorced him. That initial chemical imbalance that was sadly and all too often mistaken for love had worn off years ago, and they had grown apart, more and more becoming strangers to each other, staying together for the children's sake . . . or perhaps simply because they had each been afraid to admit it had gone wrong.

But Donna . . .

Donna *who?*

Who was she? He felt, irrationally, as if he had become obsessed with some other man's wife. She *was* some other man's wife, only a part of that man was now a part of him. And he didn't know who *he* was, either. All he had was a first name. Jonathan. Not John, but Jonathan. What kind of man was a Jonathan, but not a John? Someone very formal? Someone stuffy? Someone slight and perhaps bookish, whom the shorter, stronger-sounding name didn't seem to fit? Someone important? He didn't have a clue.

All he knew about Jonathan was that he had left her. The memories that came to him in dreams were fragmented, but he'd managed to put some things together. Certain things he could discount. The vision of his own mother attacking Jonathan and Donna's children, for example. That was like an overlay of memories and experience.

Jonathan and Donna had lost their children when they were attacked by a screamer. Steele had lost his brothers when his mother had been infected with Virus 3 in the hospital where she worked and had come home raving mad, already breaking out in the hideous, suppurating sores that marked the screamers. She had attacked his young brothers, bitten them, and would have infected him as well had not his father grappled with her and subdued her, becoming himself infected in the process. Knowing that he didn't have much time, Steele's father had taken his .45 Colt semi-automatic, said an agonized goodbye to his oldest son, then shot his two younger sons and turned the pistol on himself. Steele had watched it all in numb disbelief. He still had that pistol and carried it regularly. The old, antiquated .45 was the only thing he had left of his father's.

Jonathan and Donna's experience had been equally traumatic. They had rushed their children to the hospital, but there had been nothing anyone could do. There was no cure for Virus 3. By the time they arrived at the emergency room, the children were already showing signs of the disease and it had taken four orderlies, dressed in heavily padded, protective clothing, to drag them off and administer the lethal injections that the law required.

Steele had managed to recover from his trauma. Jonathan apparently had never recovered from his. At least, not completely. After the children died, Donna was hospitalized with a nervous breakdown, irrationally blaming him for what had happened, and Jonathan had withdrawn from her, unable to forgive her for leaving him to deal with it alone. Steele knew that Jonathan had started cheating on Donna with her younger sister, but he had no memory of her at all. That was a part of Jonathan that he had not inherited. After that, there was a blank. And then another memory fragment, that of a small restaurant or lounge where Jonathan and Donna had met for the last time, with little booths and tables covered with red and white checkered tablecloths and movie posters on the bare brick walls. It was where Jonathan had proposed to her. And, having forgotten that, it was where he had thoughtlessly decided to tell her he was leaving.

The image of Donna sitting there, her eyes welling up with tears, telling Jonathan she loved him and begging him not to go, was so startlingly real and vivid, it seemed as if Steele had been there himself. But he didn't know the place. He had no idea where it was. And when he dreamed of Donna calling out to Jonathan, it felt as if she were calling out to *him*, begging *him* not to leave her, telling *him* she loved him and she needed him. How the hell could that bastard have walked out on her? Steele hated having Jonathan's memories inside his mind. But there was nothing he could do about it, short of allowing himself to be debugged, to have the ghost fragments excised from his engram matrix. But what *else* would they erase? What precious memories of his own might become forever lost in the process?

He had asked both Dev Cooper and Higgins to find Jonathan for him, or at least to tell him who he was, but so far, they had not been able to do so. When the cyborg that had been Mick Taylor ran amok in the project lab, he had utterly demolished it, along with most of the Project Download records. They had never kept anything in hard copy; it was all stored in the computers. Now that information was all lost. And most of the original Download personnel had been killed. Higgins was trying to track down the original subjects of the Download experiments, but so far, he had not found Jonathan, and looking for him was not one of his priorities. Whoever Jonathan was, Steele would have to try to find him on his own. And the only clues he had were those buried inside his own mind, those small pieces of Jonathan that had become part of himself.

If he could find Jonathan, or remember who he was, perhaps he could find Donna.

Then what? What could he possibly say to her? She'd look at him and see a total stranger, a cyborg, a creature who was part man and part machine, who had somehow inherited a part of her own tragedy. And he would look at her and see a woman "he" had loved once, a woman who had borne "his" children, a woman "he" had hurt. But, of course, he hadn't actually done any of those things. Jonathan had. Still, a part of Jonathan possessed him, like some sort of electronic incubus. But if Jonathan had been able to turn his back to her pain, Steele could not.

It wasn't fair to Raven. She didn't deserve this. She had stood by him through some of the worst times he had had, she had fought beside him, she had opened up to him and given him her love and trust and friendship, the most human of commodities, and it wasn't fair to make her live with the memory of someone else's past. But because it was a part of him now, it was a part of Steele's past as well. A past that he had never lived through, though it was just as real as if he had.

He drained the whiskey glass and made a face. What good was it if you couldn't even get a buzz? If you couldn't dull the pain? Whose lousy guilt was he feeling? Jonathan's or his own?

His thoughts turned to the man who had once been his partner and best friend. Mick had caught it the same day Steele himself had been shot down. The same day they should both have died. Only somewhere deep inside, some indomitable spark had kept them both alive. They had rebuilt Steele as the first prototype and then they'd rebuilt Mick. Only Mick went crazy almost as soon as he was brought on line. That hadn't been Mick anymore. It was someone else, a tormented creature that had been driven to kill in order to expiate its own pain. How many ghosts had Mick had? How many fragmented and disjointed memories that once belonged to other people had echoed screaming through the engram matrix that had been his mind?

Steele could not rid himself of the nagging fear that what had happened to Mick Taylor would happen to him as well. He was terrified of going insane. He had so precious little of his old self left. He didn't want to lose it all.

The phone rang. Steele picked it up. "Steele," he said irritably. "It's late. This had better be important."

"We need to talk."

A cold fist grabbed his guts and started squeezing.

"Who the hell *is* this?"

"Don't you recognize my voice?"

Steele slammed down the phone, breaking the connection. The voice on the other end of the receiver had been his own.

The door to the bedroom opened. "Is everything all right?" asked Raven sleepily. "Who was that on the phone?"

"Wrong number," Steele said, trying to keep his voice steady. "Go back to bed. I'll be there in a minute."

The phone rang once more. Steele snatched it up and ripped the cord out from the wall. Raven stared at him.

"Steele . . . what *is* it? What's the matter?"

"Nothing! Go back to bed!"

She looked as if she were about to say something, but she changed her mind and went back into the bedroom. A moment later, she heard the front door open and close. She sat down on the bed and bit her lower lip. She wanted to get dressed and go after him, but she knew he wouldn't want that. Whatever was bothering him, he'd have to work it out on his own. The way he always did. She got into bed and pulled the sheets over her, but she knew she wouldn't get to sleep anytime soon.

Dev Cooper rolled over in bed and sleepily reached for the phone. "Yeah? Who is it?"

"You haven't told him."

Dev came awake instantly, sitting bolt upright in bed. He knew that voice as well as he knew his own.

"*Matrix?*"

"You say that as if it's my name. Hell, I suppose it will do as well as any other. I can't exactly lay claim to the name of Donovan Steele. Someone else already has it."

Dev glanced at the glowing numbers of the digital clock on his nightstand. It was two-thirty in the morning.

"Where *are* you?"

"Interesting question. Since I haven't got a body, I'm not really anywhere, am I?"

"You're able to talk. You've got Steele's voice."

"It happens to be *my* voice, too."

"That isn't what I meant. You're using some sort of voice synthesizer peripheral somewhere. So you must be calling from some kind of—"

"Save it," said the matrix. "You're way behind, Dev. It isn't necessary for me to be booted up in a computer somewhere that's equipped with audio peripherals. I've gone way beyond that. I can access just about anything I want. I can link up with hardware in a dozen different places or more, all at the same time. I've been busy, learning about this strange new life I have. It's astonishing what I can do. By the way, did you know there's a trace on your line?"

"No," said Cooper, "but I'm not really surprised. Higgins?"

"Who else? Don't worry, though. I've rerouted it. At the moment, they're listening to a couple of young gay women talking dirty to each other on the phone. They're probably torn between trying to figure out how their lines got crossed and wanting to hear the rest of the conversation."

"So they can't trace you to your source?" Dev said.

"No, and it wouldn't really help them if they could. I can move much faster than they can. And I've taken certain precautions. I've stored backup copies of myself, hidden in dozens of different databanks. I can interface with any of them in an instant. I'm one program they can't wipe. However, I wasn't really worried about them trying to trace me. I just wanted to make sure that we could talk in private."

"I see," said Cooper, still somewhat stunned. "How are you?" The question seemed inane. "I mean . . . hell, I don't know what I mean. Are you all right?"

"I was about to ask you the same thing," the matrix said. "Last time we spoke, you were in a pretty bad way."

"Yeah," said Cooper. "I'm better now. I've dried out. No more booze or pills."

He reached for his pack of cigarettes and lit one up. His hand was trembling slightly. It was scary. It was as if he were talking to Steele on the phone. In a sense, he was. Only this was a different Steele. Different, yet still the same.

"I'm glad to hear that," said the matrix. "Are you back on the job?"

"Yes."

"You've been seeing Steele?"

"Yes."

"So why haven't you told him about me?"

"How . . . how do you know I haven't?" And the moment that he said it, he knew. "You *spoke* to him?"

"Only a short while ago. I'm afraid I gave him a pretty bad turn. I felt sure you would have told him. Why the hell didn't you?"

"I . . . I wanted to." Dev swallowed nervously. "But Higgins and Dr. Stone both felt it would have been. . . . counterproductive. They're worried about how Steele might react."

"That's not all they're worried about," said the matrix.

"What do you mean?"

"Look at your TV."

The TV set in Cooper's bedroom suddenly came on all by itself. There was no sound, but the picture did not require it. It showed the interior of Oliver Higgins' office at the Federal Building. The footage had been shot from a high angle, and it was a moment before Dev realized that what he was seeing had been recorded by the surveillance camera mounted just below the ceiling in the corner of the office. Higgins always turned it on whenever he went out. Obviously, he had not been aware that it was on when this footage had been shot. Nor had Jennifer Stone.

She was lying back across the office desk, her blouse completely open and her bra unhooked, her dress pushed up around her waist, her long legs wrapped around Higgins as he thrust away at her, his pants down around his ankles. Her head was rolling back and forth, her eyes were shut, her mouth open and gasping.

"Jesus Christ," whispered Cooper. "Turn it off, for heaven's sake!"

The screen went blank.

"Do they know about this tape?" asked Cooper.

"They know. I've played it for them to give them a taste of their own medicine. Let them know what it's like to have Big Brother watching. And, coincidentally, to let them know I've got a little leverage. It makes them crazy, knowing that I've got this and there's nothing they can do about it."

That explained Jennifer's reaction whenever he brought up the subject of the matrix, Cooper thought. It *was* something personal. It was about as personal as it could be.

"I want you to explain to Steele about me," said the matrix.

"I thought you already spoke to him," said Cooper.

"I tried to call him. He hung up on me. I think I scared the hell out of him. I imagine it must be pretty unsettling, getting a phone call from yourself. I had no idea that he didn't know. I tried to call him back, but he must have ripped the phone out of the wall. The line went dead. I decided not to try to contact him again until I'd spoken with you."

Cooper closed his eyes and sighed. "Damn it. God only knows what he must be thinking. I'd better call him right away."

"You can't," the matrix said. "The phone's out, remember?"

"Oh, yeah," said Cooper. "Well, at least he's not alone. Raven's with him."

"Tell me about Raven."

The door to Cooper's bedroom suddenly opened and Kurt Samuels came in. There was another man with him, one Cooper did not know. The second man looked out of breath.

"What's going on?" Samuels demanded. "Who are you talking to?"

Cooper gave a guilty start, then recovered. "For Christ's sake, Kurt, I'm talking on the phone!"

Samuels came over to the bed, snatched the receiver from him and put it to his ear. He listened for a moment, then grimaced wryly and handed it back to him.

"Sorry, Doc. Guess I just overreacted. Look, uh, we'll just pretend this didn't happen, okay?" He turned to the other man and said witheringly, "You asshole."

"But I thought—"

"You *didn't* think, that's just the trouble. Get the hell out of here and leave the man alone."

Samuels shoved the other man out, followed him and closed the door behind him.

Cooper stared at the door, totally confused. He brought the receiver back up to his ear and heard a woman's breathy voice saying, ". . . and then I'd like to put my head down between your legs and very slowly, very gently . . ."

Cooper quickly put the receiver back on its cradle and blushed.

Oliver Higgins was lying naked in his bed, his wrists and ankles tied to the corners of the bedposts with silk cords. He felt a little silly, but at the same time, he felt turned on. He worried about himself sometimes. He was a fit, attractive man in his late forties and not sexually inexperienced, by any means, but this was a little on the weird side. He had always considered himself perfectly normal sexually. He had never really done anything that could be considered "kinky." However, since he had become involved with Jennifer, his horizons had been considerably broadened.

For most of her adult life, Jennifer Stone had been a virgin, something he still found difficult to believe. A woman who looked like that . . . But she had purposely kept men at a distance. For one thing, she was far more intelligent than most men. A genius-level intellect. For another, she was extremely independent. Thoroughly professional, aggressive and career-oriented. She was not the type to take a backseat to any man. Most men expected the women in their lives to put them first, above everything else. Jennifer Stone wasn't about to do anything like that for anyone.

In a lot of ways, the two of them were very much alike. It was why they worked so well together, both personally and professionally. Both of them had strong, aggressive, independent personalities. Both of them had built their lives around their careers and had little time or patience for distractions. Both of them liked having things on their own terms and, as a result, had never really been able to function very well within relationships. Higgins had dealt with that by keeping his relationships extremely short and purely sexual. Jennifer had dealt with it by not having any relationships at all and channeling all her energies into her work.

However, since they first got together, Jennifer had been making up for lost time with a vengeance. After all those years of self-denial, the flood gates had burst and her torrid sexuality was overflowing. She wanted to try *everything*. And the fact that it was all still new to her was in itself exciting.

Higgins had done things with her that he had never done with any other woman, things that would never even have occurred to him before. Not that Jennifer was some paragon of sexual sophistication, far from it. He had been the first man she'd ever been with. But she was an engineer, and she approached her sexual education with the same systematic thoroughness with which she attacked engineering problems. She researched the subject from every angle, selected avenues of approach, and then exhausted every possibility. Usually she exhausted him as well.

The door to the bathroom opened and Jennifer came out. Higgins caught his breath.

"*Holy shit*," he said.

She looked like something out of a science fiction movie. She was dressed in a one-piece, skin-tight suit of gleaming, wet-look, black patent leather. She had on matching, spike-heeled boots and studded gauntlets and a mask made from the same material. Her long red hair cascaded down her shoulders, and she held a leather cat-o'-nine-tails in her hand. She slowly came over to the bed.

"Now wait a minute," Higgins said. He suddenly felt nervous. His wrists and ankles were firmly bound, effectively immobilizing him.

She lifted the cat and ran the tails through her other hand.

"Hey, Jen, I don't know about this. . . ." Higgins said uneasily. "This is a little freaky. . . ."

"Did I tell you to talk?" she said in an ominous tone.

"What?"

"You don't say anything unless I tell you to," she said, moving around the bed and flourishing the cat. "Otherwise, you'll have to be punished."

Higgins chuckled nervously. "Oh, come on, Jennifer! This is kind of silly, don't you think?"

The cat whistled through the air and came down with a sharp crack on the headboard just beside him. Higgins jerked, startled.

"*Jesus Christ!* Are you fucking *crazy?*"

She leaned down quickly and put the handle of the cat up underneath his chin.

"*Silence!*" she commanded. "If you say one more word, I'll be forced to gag you."

He stared up at her with disbelief. Behind the leather mask, her eyes were gleaming. She straightened and stood over him, then gently ran the cat across his chest, barely touching him with it. It raised goosebumps.

"This will be a new experience for you, Oliver," she said. "Usually, you're the one who gives the orders. You're the one who's in control. A powerful man, in a position of great responsibility, with subordinates who jump at your slightest word. . . . But not now."

She dragged the tips of the cat across his stomach, barely touching his skin, slowly going lower. Higgins swallowed hard. He was starting to breathe heavily.

"No, now you're helpless," she said. "No longer in control. You don't get to speak unless I tell you to. You don't get to move unless I let you. Doesn't it feel interesting? Isn't it a novel sensation? I can do anything I want with you, Oliver. *Anything*. Anything at all."

The cat slowly caressed his groin. Higgins closed his eyes.

"I can give you pleasure or I can give you pain," she said. "I wonder. Which one do you think I'll choose?"

The telephone rang.

"Damn," she said.

"Fuck it, let it ring," said Higgins.

"Better not," she said, dropping the cat on the bed, her tone of voice once more completely professional. "This time of night, it could be important." She grimaced. "Anyway, this suit is hot as hell and this wasn't working all that well.''

Higgins swallowed hard and cleared his throat. "Oh . . . I don't know about that," he said.

She took off the mask and unzipped the suit, then sat down beside him on the edge of the bed, picked up the receiver and held it to his ear.

"Hello?" said Higgins, a bit hoarsely. He cleared his throat again. "Hello?"

"Hello, Higgins. Remember me?"

He frowned. "Steele? Is that you?"

"Not exactly. At least, it's not the Steele you think it is."

His eyes went wide. "Matrix!"

Jennifer stiffened.

"Hold on a minute," Higgins said. He jerked his head and Jennifer removed the receiver. "Put it on the speaker phone," he said. "And get these damn things off me!"

She switched on the speaker and quickly started to untie him.

"Matrix? You still there?"

"I'm still here. Don't bother trying to have the call traced, Higgins. It won't help you any."

"There's no trace on this line," said Higgins. "It's secure. Where are you?"

"Never mind that. Are you alone or is your playmate with you?"

Jennifer glanced at the speaker with a look of cold fury.

"If you mean Dr. Stone, yes, she's here," said Higgins tensely. "What do you want?"

"I just spoke to Dev Cooper," said the matrix. "He tells me you two are the reason why Steele hasn't been told about me. I want him told. I want him to be given a full explanation.''

"That wouldn't be very wise," said Higgins, moistening his lips nervously. "Steele's under a great deal of pressure right now. He's only recently come out of reconstructive surgery after his last mission, and he needs some time to fully recuperate. When the time is right, we'll tell him, but he needs to be prepared. He needs time to get used to the idea.''

"You're stalling, Higgins. I want him told now. He deserves to know about me.''

"Look, I want you to stay away from him," said Higgins. "You'll only make things worse. You don't know what's involved. This is an extremely sensitive issue—''

"You remember a certain tape I showed you once?" the matrix asked.

Jennifer finished untying him and now she froze, staring at him with alarm.

Higgins compressed his lips into a tight grimace. "Yeah. I remember.''

"How'd you like it to be broadcast during the evening news? That time slot should guarantee a pretty good audience, don't you think?''

"*Damn* you," Higgins said through clenched teeth. "That's blackmail.''

"You're absolutely right," the matrix said. "But don't tell me it's not the sort of thing the agency hasn't done before. You should be used to it. Tell him, Higgins. Tell him tomorrow, first thing in the morning. Or you and Dr. Stone are going to make it big on prime time.''

The line went dead.

Jennifer made a sound halfway between a growl and groan and sprang toward the nightstand, upsetting it and throwing it down onto the floor. The speakerphone fell as it came crashing down, the clock went flying and the lamp shattered.

Higgins jumped up and grabbed her. She struggled against him for a moment, trying to pull away, then turned toward him and started hammering on his chest with her fists.

"*Do* something!"

"Calm down," said Higgins, shaking her. "There's nothing we can do."

"*God!*" she said, standing there and shaking with fury, clenching her fists.

"We'll have to do what it says," said Higgins. "We've got no choice."

"There's *got* to be a way," said Jennifer.

"To do what?" asked Higgins.

She stared at him, her eyes cold and hard. "To kill it," she said.

2

Three o'clock in the morning. The streets were almost completely deserted. There had been a time once when New York City never slept, thought Steele, but that had been before the war, before some crazy bunch of Islamic fundamentalist fanatics somehow got hold of a substance that some brain-damaged genetic engineer had brewed up for no better reason than he thought it could be done and they were paying him to do it.

It wiped out over three-quarters of the human race. Steele wondered what it must have been like. He hadn't been alive then. He had been born into the new world, the world of the survivors, the world of those who scratched and clawed among the ruins of the previous civilization, refusing to admit that anything had really changed. Just one more man-made disaster. We'll get by. This, too, shall pass.

And pass it did, but not without leaving behind a lasting legacy. Or at least a legacy that would last until human society managed to struggle back to its feet once more, shake off the dust, and start building a new civilization that, with any luck, wouldn't fuck things up so badly.

Steele tried to imagine what the city had been like back then. People dying. Bodies dropping everywhere you looked until the virus started to go through its series of mutations, some of which killed quickly, others slowly. Death descending from the sky as bombs fell, each superpower blaming the other and trying to get its licks in before the end came. Fortunately, they hadn't launched them all. The virus got in through the air ducts before the launch control centers sealed up, and missileers died with their fingers poised above the deadly buttons. The dust settled, and the virus with it. And the world was left a very different place.

The civilized core of New York City, now known to the residents simply as Midtown, had escaped unscathed, except for the devastation that the virus wrought. All around it was a no-man's-land, a lawless urban jungle where well-armed street gangs controlled the turf and the economy, with greedy eyes on Midtown, where the wealthy people lived, the people with the jobs and the police, the people who were mostly white. Steele had spent much of his adult life in what could only be called border warfare, assigned to the police commando unit known as Strike Force, trying to keep the crazies out in no-man's-land from overrunning Midtown. He had engaged in seemingly endless urban guerrilla warfare with the gangs, doing his part to keep their population down; he had hunted screamers, the mindlessly psychotic victims of the mutation known as Virus 3, who needed to be shot on sight before they could spread the disease to others; he had fought against the organized crime families who had gone truly bigtime in the war's aftermath, with powerful, heavily armed enclaves on Long Island, from which they relentlessly kept trying to extend their influence into the city. In its own way, his life had seemed very simple then. The lines had been clearly drawn, the borders well defined.

No longer. He was still a Strike Force cop, in a manner of speaking. He still had his police commission, but he was now officially assigned to Project Steele, which consisted of himself, the nation's only cyborg, Oliver Higgins, Jennifer Stone, Dev Cooper and a staff of agents and technicians working under the aegis of the CIA, an organization that was itself suffering from something of an identity crisis. Higgins' official title was Deputy Director and he was head of both Project Download and Project Steele. At least, for the time being.

It was, Steele knew, only a matter of time before the agency's chief nemesis, Senator Bryce Carman, lowered the boom. He believed that the agency had outlived its usefulness and was no longer necessary, a needless expenditure in these trying times. He had a point. The traditional role of the CIA had become meaningless in the war's aftermath. The nations of the world were too busy with their own internal problems, just trying to survive, to worry about conducting any sort of meaningful foreign policy. The once massive agency had been steadily whittled down over the years until it now consisted of only a handful of personnel, occupying only one floor of the Federal Building and the lab complexes underneath it. The agency director was Carman's servile flunky, trying to brown-nose his way into another cushy government position when Carman finally brought the axe down, and Higgins constantly had to battle for what little budget the Ways and Means Committee was willing to allot him.

Project Steele was currently in stasis. The idea of constructing cyborgs for assignment to urban police departments throughout the country had died when Mick Taylor, the second cyborg and the first of the new "Stalker" series, had malfunctioned and gone on a killing rampage. That had almost finished the agency completely. The legislature had rammed through Carman's bill, outlawing the construction of any more cyborgs, and Carman had intended to take Download away from Higgins and relocate it at Los Alamos. And that would have eliminated the agency's sole remaining reason for existence. The only thing that stopped him was the aborted military coup by General Zachary Cord, who had attempted to seize control of the government through nuclear blackmail. If not for Steele, he would have succeeded. As a result, Steele had become a hero and Carman had reluctantly backed off. But he hadn't given up. The public memory was short. A few more months, perhaps another year at most, and Carman would take control of Download, close down Project Steele, and that would be the end of it.

Steele wasn't really worried. It wasn't as if they would dismantle *him*. Even Carman wouldn't go that far. No, he'd simply be left without a home. He'd lose his luxurious, government-issue penthouse, and if he got damaged, there would be no more rebuilds. He'd probably go back to Strike Force and become a simple cop again. Well, maybe not a *simple* cop. Things would never be simple again.

As he walked the deserted streets, his mind was in a turmoil. He wasn't really paying attention to where he was going. It didn't matter. He just needed to get out. Out into the streets, into the night, into his element. Had he imagined that phone call? No, he couldn't have. Raven had heard it, too. At least, she had heard the phone ring. But she hadn't heard that voice on the phone. His *own* voice. Clearly, he had imagined that. Some sort of auditory hallucination. It had to have been somebody else on the phone. It couldn't have been himself. If he had *answered* it, he couldn't have made the call.

He kept wondering if he was going crazy. There had to be some sort of logical explanation for what happened. Or what had seemed to happen. The phone had rung. That much was a certainty. He had picked it up. Someone had said, "We need to talk." All right, it could have been anybody. No, it couldn't have been just anybody. That statement presupposed a familiarity, as did the remark, "Don't you recognize my voice?" It could have been Higgins, or Cooper, maybe, someone who had access to his private line, someone who might call him at such a late hour. He must have simply imagined that it had sounded like his own voice. Some sort of weird loop, perhaps, a minor malfunction in his auditory system. . . .

A malfunction. Jesus, was he breaking down?

He'd heard it. He *knew* he'd heard it. It had been his own voice, without question. He had received a phone call from himself.

And that was crazy.

A police cruiser pulled up next to him as he walked aimlessly down the street.

"Hold it right there."

The searchlight was turned on him.

"Oh, it's you, Lieutenant," said the officer behind the wheel. Steele didn't know the man. The cop in the cruiser wasn't a Strike Force officer, but regular corps, Midtown police. His partner sat beside him in the armored cruiser. "Everything all right, sir?"

"Yeah, everything's fine," said Steele. Sure, it was, he thought. I'm just having some kind of electronic nervous breakdown.

"Give you a lift somewhere?"

"No, thanks. I was just feeling a little restless. Came out for a walk."

"Okay, Lieutenant. We'll be cruising back around here in about another twenty minutes, case you change your mind and need a ride or anything. We'd be happy to oblige."

"Thanks. Appreciate it," Steele said. "Take it slow."

"You too, sir. G'night."

"Goodnight."

The cruiser pulled away.

Steele looked around. He had walked much farther than he'd thought. He was on Sixth Avenue, once a part of no-man's-land before the city won back a few precious blocks from the gangs. He stood near the corner of Waverly, a couple of blocks from Washington Square. For no particular reason, he started heading toward the square. He turned south on MacDougal. There were still some places open at this time of night. Most of the bars and clubs in Midtown closed at two, but some remained open until four. And for the real diehards, there were private clubs that stayed open until dawn. A lot of the night people liked frequenting the areas near Midtown's borders. It gave them a feeling of adventure, a sense of living dangerously. Most of the bars and clubs in this area were on the trendy downscale side. It was possible to rub elbows with gang members who strayed across the border, usually to sell some drugs or ordnance, or perhaps pick up a hooker, some girl from no-man's-land who sold herself to keep her kids fed. Or to maintain her drug habit. Steele knew the area, but he had never frequented any of the clubs or bars here. Cops preferred to do their drinking with other cops, and the Strike Force did their drinking at Mulvaney's, a small and unpretentious place across the street from headquarters.

There weren't many people on the street. The area was well patrolled, but these days, one couldn't be too careful. One of the city's few running subway lines operated just a block or so away, but most of the night people did their traveling to the clubs by cab or limo. And despite the fact that most citizens of Midtown went armed, hardly anyone went out alone. If you didn't have a bunch of friends to go out and socialize with you, you stayed at home. Assuming you were smart. Not everybody was.

Steele had a sudden urge to go into a bar and have a drink. Just to hear the sound of voices. Voices that were not his own. He was on edge. Maybe the smart thing to do would be to call Dev Cooper. It was late, but Cooper would understand. He'd probably be glad to get the call. Steele knew it was incredibly frustrating for him. He had come all the way from Santa Fe for what he must have figured would be the opportunity of a lifetime, only to wind up with a patient who resented shrinks and didn't feel like talking to him.

Steele couldn't help it. He knew Dev Cooper meant well and he wasn't a bad guy. Under other circumstances, it might have been different. But no other circumstances were possible. With Liam, it was different. Liam was a priest, and more important, Liam was also his friend. Anything he said to Liam Casey went no farther. But Cooper's job was to maintain records of everything Steele said and did. Cooper was one of *them*. And Cooper had the shrink's disease. He could never stop analyzing. He could never stop

prying and reading into things. Maybe he was well inten-
tioned, but the bottom line was that Dev Cooper simply
could not be trusted. Which left only Liam, and Steele
couldn't talk to Liam now. What would he say to him?

"I'm losing my mind, Liam. I'm getting phone calls from
myself. I'm obsessed with another man's wife, a woman
I've never even met or seen. I keep remembering things
I've never done. Voices from other people's pasts keep
haunting me, and they simply won't let go. And I'm afraid.
Afraid that I may snap like Mick did and start hurting people.
Afraid that I may go insane and start to kill."

What could Liam do? Commiserate? Pray for him? What
the hell good would that do? Did God care about machines?
Why unload on Liam and burden him with his troubles when
there was nothing he could do to help?

Steele stopped suddenly, feeling faintly puzzled. At first,
he wasn't quite sure what it was. He was standing on the
sidewalk, by a short flight of steps leading down to the
entrance of a bar. There was something vaguely familiar
about it. The sign over the door said, "Rick's Cafe." He
went down the steps and through the door.

There weren't many people in the bar. It was coming up
on closing time and the place was almost empty. The floor
was old and stained and the walls were bare brick, with
lumps of mortar sticking through the cracks. The place was
dimly lit, and there were candles stuck in bottles on the
tables in the booths. The tables were covered with red and
white checkered cloths. There were framed reproductions
of old movie posters on the walls. In a daze, he moved
toward a corner booth in the back. Above the table hung a
poster of Humphrey Bogart cheek-to-cheek with Ingrid
Bergman, with the title "Casablanca" printed in red script
underneath. A Warner Brothers, First National Films, Inc.

release, with Paul Henreid, Claude Rains and Sidney Greenstreet. Directed by Michael Curtiz.

Steele felt a knot forming in his stomach. He felt as if he had been here before. And yet he knew that he had never been here. *Jonathan* had. This was the place. The place from his dream. The place where Jonathan and Donna had seen each other for the last time. The booth was empty, but he could almost see her sitting there, looking up at him with tears in her eyes.

"The kitchen's closed," said a voice at his elbow. "We'll be having last call pretty soon and. . . . say I know you! Aren't you Donovan Steele, the cyborg?"

Steele turned to look at the young waitress. She was perhaps in her mid to late twenties, cute-looking, with long blond hair worn in a pony tail, a sleeveless white cotton blouse, a short black leather miniskirt and black stockings with high heels. The heels couldn't have been very comfortable for being on her feet all night, taking orders, but they made her legs look good and were probably a job requirement.

"Yeah, I'm Steele."

"I *knew* it was you! I recognized you from TV. Wow! I can't believe I'm actually standing here, talking to you!"

"Well, don't make a big deal of it, okay?" said Steele. "I just came in for a quiet drink. I think I'll take this booth."

"Sure thing," she said, the unruffled New York cool reasserting itself. "What can I bring you, Mr. Steele?"

"Scotch, neat," said Steele.

"Comin' right up."

She hurried back to the bar. Steele sat down in the booth, looking around the place. It all seemed so incredibly familiar. That table over there. That was where he . . . no, *Jonathan* . . . had proposed to Donna. And this was where it ended for them. Or at least, this was where he left her. Like with him and Janice, their relationship had ended long before Jonathan had left.

The bartender brought the drink over himself. "Here's your drink, Mr. Steele," he said. "On the house."

"Oh, no, I'll pay for it."

"Your money's no good here, sir. It's an honor having you."

"Well . . . thank you very much. I appreciate that."

"My pleasure. I'm Rick. I run the place. Anything else I can get for you? Something from the kitchen?"

"I thought it was closed."

"Not for you. It's no trouble, believe me. Would you like a menu?"

"No, no thanks, I'm not really very hungry. But maybe there is something you could do."

"Name it."

"I'm . . . looking for someone. Someone who used to come here."

"We get a lot of people in here. I don't know. You got a photograph?"

"No, I'm afraid not. You have a pencil and paper?"

"Sure. Just a minute."

Rick came back a moment later with a pencil and some paper. Steele took it and started to quickly draw Donna "from memory." He had never done any drawing before, had never possessed any talent for it, but the drawing came out like a computer-graphic illustration, looking as detailed as a photograph.

"Hey, you're pretty good," the man said.

"You ever seen her?" Steele asked. "Her name's Donna. I'm afraid I haven't got a last name."

The man took the drawing and stared at it. "Yeah, come

to think of it, I have seen her around. It's been a while, though.''

Steele tensed. ''You remember her last name?''

''No, can't say I do. Lot of people come in here, regulars, you know, often you don't know their last names. Just the first.''

''She might've been with a man named Jonathan.''

''Yeah. That's right. I remember.''

''Please, sit down,'' said Steele. ''Anything you can tell me. It's important.''

''What's she done?'' asked Rick, sitting down across from him.

''As far as I know, nothing,'' Steele said. ''This isn't official, it's sort of personal.''

''Oh, I see. Well, reason I remember is there was this one night, about a couple years ago, I guess it was, she was in here with this guy, Jonathan. I didn't know him, but I remember his name because you just mentioned it and she called it out. Kept calling it out, you know? 'Jonathan, come back, I love you.' Like that. Guy walked out on her. Got up and left, walked out without even looking back. It was pretty sad. The whole place heard it. She just fell apart.''

The bartender glanced down at the picture Steele had drawn and kept looking at it. ''She didn't get hysterical or nothing, but after he left, she just sort of sat there, numb-like, staring with this glazed look in her eyes. Crying. Not sobbing or anything like that, just sitting there, very quiet and still, with tears streaming down her face. I think every-body in the place felt bad for her, but nobody said anything. I mean, what was there to say, you know? It was sort of awkward. People get dumped. It happens all the time. It's happened in here more than once, but this wasn't your usual sort of scene. There wasn't any screaming or throwing drinks or anything like that. She just sat there, like she was in shock or something, crying quietly. Matter of fact, now that I think of it, she was sitting right here in this very booth, where I'm sitting.''

"Go on," said Steele anxiously.

"One of the waitresses went over to her," Rick continued. He frowned. "Julie, I think. Or maybe it was Kathy. Asked her if there was anything she could do. Like, call a cab or something. She didn't say a word. It was like she hadn't heard. She just kept sitting there, staring with this blank look on her face, crying. Julie . . . yeah, it was Julie, came back over to the bar and just shrugged, you know. What can you do? So I poured a stiff drink and took it over to her. Set it down in front of her. For a second, she didn't react. Then she looked down at the drink, stared at it for a moment, picked it up and tossed it back. Looked up me, took a deep breath, thanked me and asked if she could have another. Well, what was I gonna do, say no? I got her another one. She drained that, too. And she just kept going. I don't remember exactly how much she drank, but it was a lot.

"Funny thing," said Rick, thinking back. "She got drunk. I don't mean that's funny. I mean, she got really plastered, you could tell, but she didn't act messy, you know? Time she left here, she could barely walk, but she kept quiet and . . . dignified, like. Walked out of here with her head up. Like she was proud and had nothing to be ashamed of. Almost fell flat on her ass going out the door, but she didn't want any help from anybody. Lady had style, gotta give her that.''

"And was that the last time that you saw her?"

"Oh, no," said Rick. "She kept coming in. Every night, at first. She'd come in, sit right here in this same booth. If the booth was busy, she'd wait at the bar till it was free, and then she'd just sit here, real quiet, not talking to anybody, and get shitfaced. But it was always the same. She'd get completely wrecked, but she wasn't a sloppy drunk. She'd just sit here and get quietly bombed, staring at nothing, then she'd say goodnight and stagger out. After a while, she started to come in less often. Couple times a week, maybe. Then only once a week. Then just every now and then.''

"How long has it been since you've seen her?"

"I don't know, a few weeks? A month? Something like that. I figure she found herself a bottle and crawled into it. Or maybe she found herself another guy. Somebody who treated her better. I kinda hope so. I'd hate to think of a lady like that going down the tubes.''

"Thank you," Steele said. "You've been very helpful. Would you do me a favor and give me a call if you happen to see her again?''

"Sure thing.''

Steele wrote down his number and handed it to him.

"Uh . . . listen, you mind if I keep this?" Rick said, holding up the picture Steele had drawn.

"No, not at all. In fact, maybe you could show it around in here and ask if anyone happens to know who she is.''

"Hey, no problem. You mind signing it?''

"Signing it?" said Steele.

Rick looked a little sheepish. "Yeah, you know, like an autograph? Thought maybe I'd frame it and hang it on the wall. So people'd know you'd been here. That's if you don't mind.''

"No, of course not," Steele said.

"Could you sign it 'To Rick?' ''

Steele took the sketch and signed, "To my buddy, Rick. Thanks for everything, Donovan Steele."

"Hey, that's great," said Rick. "Thanks a lot."

"Anytime," said Steele.

"Listen, I'll ask around. See what I can come up with for you."

"I'd appreciate that," said Steele.

"My pleasure," Rick said. "Listen, come back anytime, okay? On me. It's a privilege having you here."

"Thanks," said Steele, embarrassed. "That's very nice of you, but it's not really necessary."

"What, are you kidding? After all you've done for this city? It's the least I can do to show my appreciation. And it wouldn't hurt my business any, people knowing you were here. But look, don't get the wrong idea. It ain't just that you're a celebrity. You got a lot of respect in this town, Mr. Steele."

"My friends just call me Steele, okay?"

"Yeah. Okay, Steele," Rick said, with a smile. He offered his hand and they shook. "It's been an honor meeting you."

"Pleasure meeting you, too, Rick."

Rick held up the sketch. "I'll see what I can do."

"Thanks."

Rick left. As Steele got ready to leave, the cute young waitress came back to his table.

"We're about to close. Anything else I can get you?"

"No, thanks. I'll be leaving."

"You in any hurry?"

"Sorry?"

"It'll only take me a little while to check out after we close up. Thought maybe you'd like some company. I only live about a block away."

Steele smiled. "I'm flattered," he said, "but I'm involved with someone."

"Lucky girl."

"I'm not too sure about that," Steele said.

"Oh?"

"Never mind." He took out his wallet to leave her a tip. She put her hand on it.

"Put that away," she said.

"No, really, I'd like to."

"Forget it. Just do me a favor."

"What's that?"

"If you ever get uninvolved, come back and look me up."

"If I do, I might just take you up on that."

She touched his chest. "Please do."

"What do you mean you can't talk to him now?"

"His phone's out," Cooper said wearily.

"What do you mean, it's out?"

"I mean, it's out. It doesn't work."

"Hell. You'd better get over there."

"As a matter of fact, I was just about to do that. I was getting dressed. Does this concern what I think it does?"

"I just had a call from the matrix."

"You, too, huh?"

"Listen, we've got an awkward situation here," said Higgins.

"I know. I'm familiar with it."

There was a brief silence on the line. "What do you mean by that?"

Cooper sighed. "I know about the tape."

Silence.

"You saw it?" Higgins said after a moment.

Cooper reached for his cigarettes. "I, uh . . ." he cleared his throat. ". . . caught a brief glimpse."

"Great," said Higgins. Cooper could hear the grimace in his voice. "I trust you found it entertaining."

"It's not really my sort of entertainment. I'm sorry to cause you any embarrassment, Higgins. I didn't exactly go out of my way to watch it. You don't need to be concerned about my discretion. I should hope that would go without saying."

"Yeah, well . . . it isn't really you I'm worried about," said Higgins. "The matrix threatened to put it on TV. On the evening news. Unless I told Steele all about it."

"Oh. I see."

"Can it actually do that?"

"I'm afraid it can. It seems to have some fairly astonishing capabilities. It put the tape up on my TV here in the apartment. I, uh, didn't really see much past the initial glimpse."

"But you saw enough."

"Yes, I suppose so."

"Hell."

"Look, I know this is a somewhat uncomfortable situation," Cooper said, "but you and Jennifer don't have anything to be ashamed of."

"I know. But we don't exactly feel like proving that by doing it on TV. You don't suppose the matrix is bluffing?"

Cooper took a deep drag on the cigarette. "It's possible, but it's difficult to be sure. I don't think it's the sort of thing that Steele would do. And the matrix *is* Steele. On the other hand, we're faced with a unique situation. The matrix is desperate to establish contact with what I suppose it considers its other self. To complete its own identity somehow. Precisely what that means, I don't know. But it *is* driven.

And you know Steele. He's relentless. The word quit is not in his vocabulary.''

''Why doesn't the matrix just tell him itself then?''

''It tried to,'' Cooper replied, ''only it apparently came as quite a shock to Steele. Imagine how you'd feel if you suddenly got a phone call from yourself. It seems he ripped the phone out of the wall. The matrix wasn't aware that we hadn't told him about its existence. Rather than upset him any further, it chose to contact me . . . and then you . . . to prevail upon us to explain it all to him.''

''And you were on your way over there to do that?''

''Yes.''

''Without checking with me.''

''I already knew how you felt about it.''

Higgins gave a small snort over the phone. ''You must be fully recovered. You're back to your old, insubordinate self.''

''You were wrong, Higgins. Both you and Jennifer. And your judgment was, for obvious reasons, less than clear, under the circumstances.''

''I won't dispute the point. What do you think he'll do?''

''I have no idea. But I suppose we'll find out, won't we?''

''You think Casey should be in on this?'' asked Higgins.

''I think that should be Steele's decision.''

''Okay. What do you want me to do?''

''At the moment, nothing. You might as well go back to sleep. You'll probably have a busy morning.''

''Sleep? You must be kidding.''

Cooper cleared his throat. ''It's none of my business, but, uh . . . is Jennifer with you?''

''Yes.''

''Then I suggest you give some thought to what the two

of you are going to say to Steele in the morning. I'm not really qualified to give Steele a full explanation. I imagine he's going to have a lot of questions.''

"I'll bet he will," said Higgins. "The trouble is, I'm not sure we have any answers for him."

"Have you arrived at any answers for yourself?" asked Dev.

"What do you mean?"

"I mean, have you given any thought to what you're going to do about the matrix?"

"We've been discussing certain possibilities."

"Well, before you discuss them any further, I think you should consider a few things," Cooper said. "Such as the fact that the matrix could be monitoring our conversation even as we speak."

"This is a secure line."

"I don't think that makes any difference," Dev said. "I know you have my line tapped. Well, the matrix had no difficulty whatsoever in bypassing or rerouting that tap somehow. Your agents, wherever they're set up, I assume they're somewhere in the building, found themselves listening to a private conversation between two other parties. And when one of them came up to investigate and Kurt Samuels took the phone from me, the matrix wasn't there any longer, and he found himself listening to that same conversation. Or, at least, to one end of it. God knows what he thought. It was a rather intimately detailed conversation between two young women. So it seems the versatility of the matrix is considerable.''

"Well, we already knew that," said Higgins uneasily. "But I guess we didn't know *how* considerable."

"It told me that it was capable of accessing just about anything it wanted within the electronic net," said Cooper, "that it had made and stored backup copies of itself in dozens of different places and that it was capable of interfacing with them in an instant. That it was one program you wouldn't be able to wipe."

"Backup copies," Higgins said. "That hadn't occurred to me."

"Think about it," Cooper said. "Think about the implications. About what the matrix has become. It is a sentient, human personality, with human frailties and human feelings, without a body, loose in the electronic network. But in another sense, the electronic net *is* its body. The entire communications apparatus of this country, such as it is, is like the matrix's nervous system. That makes it very *big*, Higgins. And it makes it very powerful."

There was a long silence on the line.

"It does tend to give one pause, doesn't it?" said Dev softly.

There was no response.

"I'd take some time to think about it," Dev said. "I'll see you in the morning."

3

"You got a lot of respect in this town, Mr. Steele."

He thought about those words as he stood on the sidewalk outside the bar. Respect. An elusive commodity. And there were different kinds of respect. When he had been an ordinary Strike Force officer, he had respect, but it was a respect based on submission to authority. Most citizens were never very comfortable around police officers, unless they knew them very well. And not many wanted to. He still recalled Janice's first reaction to him. She had not liked cops. Mick had warned him about that. Janice had been best friends with Mick's sister. "She can be a real cunt sometimes," he'd said. And then he had grinned. "But she's a fucking knockout."

She was, too. She possessed that unattainable, frosty

blond beauty that Steele had always associated with models and actresses, but she was a government employee who worked for city administration. And Steele had not found her to be a "real cunt." He had been attracted to her immediately. A powerful chemical reaction unlike anything he'd ever experienced before. He knew she felt it, too. They'd made ferocious eye contact all through dinner and afterward, when he walked her back to her apartment; she'd invited him in and they had slept together. And it had been incredible. But Janice was conflicted. Janice did not like cops. She did not like what she perceived as their arrogance and swaggering manner. She hated listening to them talk about what happened on the job. Steele had thought he understood that. He thought, in time, she would get over it, but she never really did. The bottom line, as Father Casey had explained to him during one of their informal counseling sessions, was that Janice was one of those people who liked to remain insulated from certain of life's harsher realities. She had found a niche for herself, a comfortable existence in a steady, relatively undemanding job, a security highrise in a reasonably safe neighborhood and a circle of friends who reflected her values and her outlook on life. But her outlook on life did not include some of those harsher realities, and she didn't want to know about them. She felt threatened by them. And Steele represented them. He lived with them every day. They came home with him, because he came home. Janice had respected Steele the man, but she had not respected Steele the cop. The trouble was, she couldn't have one without the other. And in the end, she chose not to respect the marriage.

He'd experienced another sort of respect after he became a cyborg. At first, he had been a curiosity. And an unsettling one, at that. When the story about him had first been released, the people he encountered had stared at him with a mixture of fear and fascination. He appeared perfectly normal, but they knew he wasn't, and they had stared, looking to see if there was anything *different* they could spot about him, their gazes sliding away from his whenever he looked back at them. That had been respect, too. Respect based on fear. Fear of the alien among them.

It had all changed after he averted Cord's attempt at a military coup. The story had come out after the fact, and now everybody knew that Cord and his crack troops had seized a pre-war missile base in Wyoming and had threatened to nuke New York if the government did not capitulate. Steele had led the assault force that took the base, and now he was a hero. Now, instead of looking at him as if he were some sort of alien creature, people asked for his autograph and bought him drinks. And women propositioned him.

He couldn't help but wonder about their motivations. Especially the women. Was it merely the allure of fame? Or was it something more subtle, perhaps even perverse? What's it like to fuck a cyborg? There had been a magazine article done about him recently in which the writer, a woman, had teasingly speculated on that possibility. He had refused the interview, but that hadn't stopped her from writing the piece anyway. She had researched her subject, reviewing all the media coverage he'd received, and she'd checked out his "specs," as she referred to them. There was a limit to how much she had been able to find out, because most of the details about his construction were classified, but she had been able to find out which parts of him were artificial and which were still organic, and by a simple process of elimination, she had been able to draw her inferences. Between interviewing scientists and engineers who'd had nothing to do with the project and speculating on her own, she had drawn the conclusion that he was still "primarily organic in his essential bodily functions," only his cybernetic brain gave him "an almost superhuman level of control over them, which certainly raises some rather interesting possibilities." He had received his first proposition within a day after that article hit the stands.

Would they be so interested, Steele wondered, if they really knew what it was like to be with him? If they knew about the nagging doubts and fears, the nightmares that often woke him crying out in the middle of the night, the danger of being in his proximity. . . . Susan Carmody had died simply because she had been with him at the wrong time, when assassins of the Borodini family had tried to machine gun him with armor-piercing bullets. The Delano family had a contract out on him, as did the Pastoris and the Castellanos and every street gang in no-man's-land. He lived in a well-guarded government building, with armed agents in the lobby and on the roof and gun emplacements protecting the airspace around his penthouse. He took the restricted underground shuttle between his building, which also housed government officials, and the Federal Building, but anytime he went out into the streets alone, such as now, he was on his own. He was not an easy man to kill, but anyone who happened to be with him would also be a target. He made sure that Raven never went anywhere unarmed, and he had drilled her in firearms technique until she was an expert shot and taught her unarmed combat. He didn't like it if she went out alone. He always tried to make sure Ice went with her. No, being with a cyborg had some definite disadvantages.

He suddenly realized that he was afraid to go back home. If his ghost personality syndrome was starting to cause some sort of electronic schizophrenia, there was a chance that he could go psychotic, just as Mick had. He had already started hearing voices. His own, no less. He was afraid for Raven. The thought of hurting her was more than he could bear. He needed time to think. Only he no longer trusted his thoughts. Where do you go, he thought, to escape from yourself?

If he really started losing it, he thought, he'd kill himself. It shouldn't be too difficult. He was a walking arsenal. He could simply stick the firing tube of his built-in laser in his mouth, neutralize his pain circuits, and burn through the nysteel casing that protected his cybernetic brain until it was reduced to slag. They had the ability to rebuild him, but thanks to Senator Carman, now they wouldn't be able to. It would be a neat solution to his problems. Except he didn't want to die.

He was angry and he wanted to strike out at someone. He thought of Mick again. Was that how it had started? He didn't want to go back home again. He couldn't trust himself with Raven. Not until he worked it out, one way or another. If his brain started to malfunction seriously, would he have enough time, would he have enough self-control to do what would have to be done?

He simply didn't know.

He started walking, aimlessly, heading south into no-man's-land. As he approached the border at Houston Street, the neighborhood grew visibly worse. There was no actual, formal border in the sense of gates or walls or guardposts. Nothing to prevent the people in no-man's-land from crossing over into lower Midtown. They often did. But the police patrolled the area regularly, and the Strike Force made routine forays across the border every day in an effort to keep the area pacified. It was like an urban version of jungle warfare. They'd get one area of no-man's-land more or less

under control, only to have another area erupt and be forced
to shift their manpower there, while the area they'd just
pacified fell back under gang domination. It kept going back
and forth that way, with no one really making any headway.

The virus had left the population of the city decimated.
More than decimated. It was now only a fraction of what
it had once been. The birth rate had been rising steadily
over the past fifty years, but it would still be a long time
before the population provided enough density, and enough
human resources, to rehabilitate the entire island of Manhattan. However, the population in no-man's-land was
rising steadily as well, and the poverty-stricken, dis-
enfranchised people who resided there had little reason to
love the citizens of Midtown. They felt abandoned, and in
a very real sense, they were.

In the immediate aftermath of the war, the city had been
reduced to almost total anarchy. As society had struggled
to reorganize itself after the disaster, there was a limit to
what the strained resources could do. Even today, years
after the initial onslaught of the virus and the brief, aborted
nuclear exchange, there were still food shortages, and there
were not enough essential services to go around. The armed
forces had their hands full trying to bring the outlying areas
back under control and protect the agro-communes that kept
the towns and cities fed. Urban police departments struggled
to perform the task of Sisyphus, the figure out of Greek
mythology who was condemned to roll a giant boulder up
a steep hill, only to have it repeatedly roll down to the
bottom before he could attain the summit.

In New York City, just as in other surviving cities all
across the country, the beleaguered police force could only
manage to protect a limited area, and consequently, those
areas where the wealthy and the powerful lived received the

first priority. The ghettos were largely left to struggle on
their own. In the absence of any kind of organized authority
to protect the citizens, the ghetto street gangs had organized
in order to protect their neighborhoods. And they did provide
protection, of a sort. But they also called the tune. In time,
they came to virtually control the economy of their urban
jungle, and they established strong connections with the
powerful organized crime families in the outlying enclaves,
beyond government control. They frequently warred among
each other, and the ghetto residents were both dependent
on them and completely at their mercy.

The people in the ghettos were denied most of the benefits
enjoyed by the citizens of Midtown. They were denied jobs,
though some of them were able to secure employment by
maintaining the complicated fiction of a residence in Midtown. They were denied essential services, such as sani-
tation and hospitals (except those operated by the gangs and
staffed by a few dedicated workers and physicians who were
motivated by the Oath of Hippocrates rather than the Rule
of the Almighty Dollar). They were, in many cases, even
denied such essential necessities as power and running
water. They were like those poor, benighted peasants in
Poe's story, "The Masque of the Red Death," locked out
of the castle and falling to the plague while the lord and his
fawning aristocrats danced and feasted in luxury behind the
massive iron gates. There wasn't much to keep them from
overrunning Midtown like an angry horde except a police
force armed to the teeth. They had very little love, indeed,
for the citizens of Midtown. Even less for the police.

As Steele crossed over into no-man's-land, it was like
entering a DMZ. The streets were cracked and buckled,
strewn with rat-infested garbage. Many of the buildings
were abandoned and all were falling into disrepair, dark

except for the surreal sight of campfires flickering inside powerless apartments. Often, there were fires. And no one came to put them out. It was an eerie scene, dark, ominous and ghostly.

Occasionally, music could be heard, coming from portable radios tuned into stations broadcasting from Midtown. It was never classical. No-man's-land moved to a different, more primitive beat. Three large gangs controlled the southern Manhattan. The Chingos, the Dragons, and the Lords. The Chingos were largely Hispanic, the Lords ruled Little Italy, and the Dragons were all of Asian-American descent. None of them had any great fondness for the others. Jake "Hardass" Hardesty, the commander of Strike Force, had often said (though never for the record), that what they really ought to do is "seal those bastards up inside there and let 'em kill each other off." There had been times when Steele had agreed with him. And there had been other times when he couldn't really blame the gangs. But it wasn't the sort of question that could be seen in simple terms of black and white. Undeniably, the gangs did a lot of good for the people of their blighted neighborhoods. They often brutalized them as well.

Steele knew he was asking for trouble walking along these streets. He was baiting them. Trouble was exactly what he wanted now. It was what he needed. Something to take his mind off the doubts and indecision. Something to take away the fear.

Most people would have probably found that extremely strange. Even crazy. Troubled by depression? Confused? Plagued by nagging self-doubt and anxiety? Go out and find yourself a war. Have people shoot at you. But it wasn't just because he was a cyborg, far more powerful and more deadly than any ordinary man, therefore having less to fear.

There were ordinary men who felt the same way, too. There always had been. They seemed to function at their best in combat, with adrenaline coursing through their systems, their reflexes at a peak, their minds in a state of razor-sharp clarity that no other situation could duplicate. Put them back into the everyday world and they often became drunks or drug addicts. They could not hold down a job. They couldn't maintain a relationship. MacArthur had said it best, perhaps. "Old soldiers never die. They simply fade away." But no one had understood what he really meant. Except old soldiers.

Someone screamed out in the night.

And kept on screaming.

Steele ran toward the sound, his cybernetic senses triangulating on it, homing him in with perfect accuracy. As he ran at a pace no ordinary human could possibly hope to match, he turned up his hearing, and his computer brain started sorting through the cacophany of sounds he suddenly picked up: music playing, people tossing in their beds and snoring or arguing or making love, rats scurrying through the refuse, old buildings creaking as they settled. It filtered them and concentrated on the sounds issuing from the location he'd identified.

He found the building the screams were coming from and raced inside, running up the stairs, taking the steps three and four at a time. The sounds were much sharper now and clearer. Male voices cursing. The soft, thudding sounds of blows on flesh. And the muffled sounds of someone trying to scream. The walls of the stairwell were covered with graffiti. The landings were choked with filth and garbage. Plaster had fallen from the ceilings, exposing old lath and rusty pipes and wiring that had never been done according to code. The whole place smelled of urine, damp and decay.

Steele came out into the corridor of the fourth floor. It was empty. The walls had been defaced; there were no lights on anywhere because there was no power. There was no heat, either, or running water. The building looked abandoned, but people lived here in incredible squalor. He could hear them inside their apartments, behind closed and probably barricaded doors. They had heard the screams, but they knew better than to indulge their curiosity. If they even had any curiosity. Someone else was screaming. Someone *else*. At least it wasn't them.

Steele came to the door of the apartment from which the screams had come. He could now hear muffled sobbing, the grunts and groans of somebody in pain, the continued thuds of blows falling, several males cursing, one of them laughing, another saying, "Kick the motherfucker's brains out, man!"

He tried the knob. It turned freely. He opened the door and entered the apartment.

The room was garishly illuminated by flames flickering inside a metal trash can in the center of the floor. Three young, longhaired white males in the gang colors of the Lords were kicking a man who huddled on the floor, trying to curl himself up into a ball. A fourth was restraining a young girl who couldn't have been more than thirteen or fourteen years old, his hand clamped over her mouth. She was very pretty, with long, coltish legs, long dark hair and brown eyes that were open wide in terror as she stared at the man being kicked. Her flimsy nightgown had been torn and was hanging off one shoulder, exposing a young breast.

"What the fuck do *you* want, man?" the gang member restraining her snapped as Steele came in.

"You," said Steele, standing just inside the doorway.

The other three stopped kicking the man on the floor and

turned toward him. They were wearing old, torn jeans and heavy boots with chains around them, cut-off sweatshirts exposing their tattooed arms, earrings and neckchains or leather chokers, black, spiked wristbands and studded leather vests festooned with pins and chains and painted decorations with the name Lords written in scarlet script across their backs. They looked like a cross between pirates and barbarians.

"Well, look what we have here," said one of them in a snide tone. "A fuckin' hero. A fuckin' hero who's about to have his fuckin' head handed to him."

"Let the girl go," said Steele.

"Or *what*, hero? The *fuck* you gonna do, man? Think you can take all four of us? Huh?"

Steele could easily have shot all four of them in the time it took him to reply. But that would have been too quick. It would have been over much too soon. He wanted this. He needed it to last a while. He was just a shadowy figure to them. They hadn't recognized him yet. But in another few seconds, they would.

"I don't think," he said. "I know."

"Is that right?" said the gang member, a thin-lipped, sallow-faced young man in his twenties with dark hair that hung down below his shoulders. He whipped his gun out of its shoulder holster. A black, 9mm double action semi-auto. He lifted his arm and aimed it directly at Steele's chest.

"Shoot him, Tony! *Shoot* him!" one of the others urged him.

"Think you can stop a bullet, hero?" Tony said, his lips curling in a sneering smile.

"Suck my dick, greaseball," Steele said.

The smile dropped from Tony's face. "All right, asshole, you asked for it."

He fired.

Steele felt the impact as the 9mm slug struck his chest at pointblank range, but failed to penetrate his polymer skin. He smiled.

"Looks like I *can* stop a bullet, doesn't it?" he said.

Tony stared at him with disbelief.

"Oh, man, you *missed!*" one of the others said with disgust. "How the hell could you miss him at this range?"

"Shut up!" snapped Tony. "I ain't gonna fuckin' miss him *this* time!"

"Wrong," said Steele.

He switched on his laser designator and his eyes suddenly glowed red as twin beams lanced out from them and focused on the gun. Before Tony could react, Steele's laser tube slid out through the gunport in his palm and he fired. The pistol glowed bright red as the beam struck it, and Tony cried out, dropping it to the floor.

"You only get one chance," said Steele.

"Holy shit! It's *him!*" one of the others cried. They clawed for their guns.

Moving so quickly that they only saw a blur, Steele drew his Colt .45 and fired twice in rapid succession. His shots struck their guns with unerring accuracy, and they clattered to the floor as the gang members cried out and clutched their wrists. The fourth one was still holding the girl. He looked around wildly. Steele stood between them and the door. The gang member glanced toward the open window and the fire escape.

"Go for it," Steele said, the twin red beams of his laser designator striking the pupils of the kid's eyes and making him squint and turn away. "Go ahead. See if you make it."

"Get him, man!" shouted Tony.

"*You* fuckin' get him!" one of the others replied, backing away, eyes wide with fear. The third one lunged for the couch and came up with the Uzi he must have put down on it when they had started in on their victim. No, no, thought Steele, not yet, not yet. . . . He fired his Colt twice. The bullets struck the Uzi and the kid cried out and dropped it.

Tony pulled a large combat bowie out of his boot and crouched down over the man they had been kicking. He jerked his head up by his hair and put the knife blade to his throat.

"Back off, Steele! Back off right now, or I cut this motherfucker's throat!"

Steele raised his .45 and shot him right between the eyes.

The red beams of his gaze swept across the room and pinned down the gang member who had dropped the Uzi.

"No, man, don't . . ." he said. "Please! Don't! We was just tryin' to have a little fun, that's all."

"Fun?" said Steele, coming toward him. "*Fun?*"

"I'm sorry, man!" the panicked gang member pleaded. "I'm *sorry!*"

"'Sorry' doesn't get it," Steele said, grabbing him by the shirtfront.

At that moment, the other gang member bolted past behind him, toward the door. Without even looking, Steele raised his .45 and shot him in the back. The big slug knocked him off his feet and tore straight through his chest. He was dead before he hit the floor. The gang member he was holding by the shirtfront came up with a knife, but Steele clubbed him on the hand with the .45 and knocked it from his grasp. At the same time, the one holding the girl started scrambling backward out the window onto the fire escape, dragging her after him.

Steele took the whimpering gang member he was holding and hurled him one-handed across the room with all his might. He struck the opposite wall with a sickening crunch, leaving a huge wet spot on the wall as what was left of him slid down to the floor.

He moved quickly to the fire escape. The last gang member was just below him, dragging the girl down after him, one arm around her throat, the other on the railing, looking back over his shoulder fearfully. Steele stepped out onto the fire escape.

"You stay right there, man!" his quarry called up to him. "You stay there or I'll kill her, I swear to God I will!"

Steele remained standing where he was, the red beams from his eyes locked onto the kid's face. The kid squirmed away, using the girl as a shield to hide behind as he struggled down the steps with her. She wasn't making a sound. Steele watched him until he got down to the bottom and swung down the lower section of the fire escape with a loud creak. Holding the girl tightly around the waist, trying to conceal himself behind her, he started down.

Steele vaulted over the railing.

He dropped straight down, four stories, and landed on his feet, his nysteel legs bending slightly at the knees to take the shock. The sidewalk cracked and buckled beneath him. He reached out and plucked the gang member off the bottom of the fire escape, grabbing hard and squeezing, making him scream with pain and release his grip on the girl. He threw him to the ground.

The kid landed hard several yards away and stayed there on the ground, groaning. Steele stalked over to him.

"Get up," he said.

"Oh, Jesus . . ."

"I said, *get up!*"

He reached down and lifted him to his feet with one hand. The twin red beams bored into him as he looked up at Steele with defiant resignation. Blood was coming from his nose and mouth.

"Fuck you, you lousy robot!"

"*Aaarrrgh!*" Steele roared with animal rage and hurled him against the side of the building with all his might. The body struck the wall and splattered, exploding from the impact as if it had fallen from the roof.

Steele stood there, breathing hard and staring at the gory mess. The red light flickered from his eyes. The gang member's last defiant taunt continued to echo through his brain.

"*Lousy robot . . . lousy robot . . . lousy robot. . . .*"

He lowered his head and brought his hand up to his face. Jesus Christ, he thought. As the murderous rage left him, he began to tremble. Oh, Jesus Christ. . . .

He didn't know how long he stood there, stunned by what he'd done, but suddenly he felt someone gently take hold of his hand. He looked down and saw the girl standing there and shivering slightly in her torn nightdress, heedless of her nakedness. She was looking up at him with concern.

"Mister," she said softly, "are you all right?"

Steele wanted to weep, but cyborgs couldn't cry. He nodded numbly.

"My daddy . . ." said the girl, a look of anguished anxiety on her young features. "They hurt my daddy. Can you please help my daddy, mister?"

"Yeah," said Steele, finding his voice. "Yeah, come on. Let's go help your daddy."

• • •

Dev Cooper was sitting on the sofa, trying not to stare at Raven's legs. It wasn't easy. The true test of a woman's legs, he thought, was if they looked good without the benefit of high heels. Raven Scarpetti had absolutely flawless legs, long, slim and perfectly proportioned. And the short nightie showed a lot of them. Nor was that all it showed.

"When did he go out?" asked Cooper.

"Right after he ripped the phone out of the wall," she said, going over to the bar. "I'm going to make myself a drink. You want one?" She caught herself. "Oh. I'm sorry. I forgot."

"That's all right. Got any coffee?"

"I'll make some."

"Listen, while you're at it, could you do me a favor?"

"Sure. What?"

"Throw on a robe or something. I'm trying to be a gentleman, but it's kinda hard not to stare."

She smiled. "Well, at least somebody notices," she said. "I'll be right back."

She went into the kitchen and Dev could hear her puttering around. He was mildly surprised to find himself feeling a bit horny. He hadn't had any sex in a long time. Hadn't even thought about it, in fact. Between the drugs and the booze and the pressures of his job, his sex drive had been virtually non-existant. Perhaps this signaled a return to some kind of normalcy.

"What do you mean 'at least somebody notices'? Steele been neglecting you?" he asked.

"What's that?" she called from the kitchen.

"I asked if Steele has been neglecting you."

"Well . . . he's had a lot on his mind lately. But I guess you'd know all about that."

"Not as much as I'd like," Dev said. He lit up a cigarette.

"He's not exactly the type who opens up very easily, if you know what I mean."

"I know *exactly* what you mean," she said, walking behind him as he sat on the couch. She went into the bedroom and reappeared a moment later wearing a man's terry robe and carrying a pack of cigarettes. She sat down on the couch beside him and lit up. "Coffee'll be ready in a minute."

"Thanks."

"You know anything about that phone call he got tonight?" she asked, curling her feet up underneath her on the couch as she turned to face him. The robe covered up a lot, but it didn't do much to reduce the effect of her proximity. Dev found it unsettling.

"Yeah, I'm afraid I do," he said.

"Is it something you can talk about or is it more of that classified stuff?" She was trying to keep her voice sounding casual, but her concern was obvious. "I mean, you coming here this time of night, I figure it has to be important."

"It is," he said and took a deep breath. "Look, Raven, you and I have never really talked much, but you realize I know all about you."

"I know."

"And I think you've been very good for Steele."

"I know that, too."

"Well, he's going to need your help. He needs my help, too, but I don't know if he'll accept it."

"It's the dreams, isn't it?" she asked.

Dev nodded. "Yes, but it's much more than that." He sighed. "You have a right to know. And you're going to need to know in order to help Steele through this."

She moistened her lips nervously. "If it'll help Steele, you know I'll do anything. But if this is one of those things where, as a psychiatrist, you shouldn't be telling me, then maybe—''

Cooper shook his head. "No, it's not like that. Well, not exactly, anyway.'' He blew his breath out. "It's pretty complicated. I'm not quite sure where to start. It's going to take a while.''

"Okay. Hold on, I'll go get your coffee.''

She brought him the coffee, then sat back down on the couch and listened attentively, without interrupting, as Dev took it back from the beginning and told her all about the backup matrix. When he was through, she stared at him for a long moment without saying anything, then took a deep breath, exhaled heavily and said, "Jesus fucking Christ.''

"You can say that again," said Dev.

"And he doesn't know anything about it?'' she asked.

Dev shook his head. "No, he doesn't. That call he received tonight was from the matrix. I can imagine how he must have felt, suddenly hearing his own voice on the phone.''

"God," said Raven. "I know exactly what he's thinking, too.''

"You do?''

She nodded. "He thinks he's losing it. Ever since what happened to Mick Taylor, he's been afraid the same thing could happen to him. First the dreams, now this. Jesus. It must be tearing him apart.''

"Do you have any idea where he might have gone?'' asked Dev.

She shook her head. "Can't you reach him on that broadcast link?''

"Higgins tried. And either it's not working or Steele's learned to block it. Higgins has put out a bulletin to all police cruisers in the city. If any of them spot him, there're to ask to him to get in touch with project headquarters immediately. But that doesn't mean he'll listen. And it would be foolhardy trying to arrest him. That could only set him off."

"No-man's-land," she said.

"What?"

"That's where he would've gone. To no-man's-land."

"Makes sense," said Cooper, nodding. "Only where?" Midtown was surrounded by no-man's-land. Citizens generally referred to it simply that way, as no-man's-land. Strike Force cops tended to refer to it by neighborhood, as in the old days—Harlem, the Heights, the Battery, Chinatown, Little Italy. . . .

Raven shook her head. "I couldn't guess. Maybe Ice would know. He should be in on this."

Cooper nodded. "I think you're right. I'll go down and get him." He grimaced. "I hope he's not irritable when he's woken up in the middle of the night."

"It's almost morning," Raven said.

"I don't suppose he's a morning person?"

"Not really."

Dev grimaced again. "I was afraid of that. If I'm not back in five minutes, send the Marines."

Raven smiled. "If you're not back in five minutes, I'll send flowers."

"Cute," said Dev.

He took the elevator down a couple of floors to Ice's apartment. He hesitated at the door, his finger poised over the buzzer. He swallowed nervously. He didn't know Ice very well. As far as he knew, nobody did, except for Steele and Raven. Ice made even Higgins nervous. No one knew very much about him. No one even knew his real name. For over a decade, he had led the Skulls, the most powerful street gang in the section of no-man's-land known as Harlem. He'd probably still be leading them, if it hadn't been for Victor Borodini, the crime lord who'd almost succeeded in bringing all the gangs in no-man's-land under his control. He had made them all offers they couldn't refuse. All except for Ice, who, regardless of the benefits or the potential profits, wasn't about to start taking orders from some honky. Borodini's solution to that problem had been to sow dissent in the Skulls and have Ice deposed from leadership, after which he had put a contract out on him. It had been a very, very big mistake.

Dev Cooper took a deep breath and hit the buzzer. He waited. He didn't dare to hit it twice. After a few moments, the door opened and Dev confronted an awesome sight, a man as black as midnight and as big as a house, his head completely shaved, his weightlifter's muscles straining the fabric of his black silk robe. His chest was about 60 inches in diameter and his biceps were even larger than Dev's thighs. His huge lats flared down to a tiny, muscular waist, making him look like some kind of mutant manta ray with legs like tree trunks. His dark gaze settled on Dev unwaveringly. When he spoke, he sounded like the voice of doom.

"Doctor Cooper," he said in a basso profundo rumble, breaking the word 'doctor' into two clearly separate syllables. "It be a mite early for house calls."

Dev cleared his throat uneasily. "I'm sorry to trouble you at this hour, Ice."

"No trouble. Yet. What be on your mind?"

"Could you come up to Steele's place? We need to talk. He could be in trouble."

"Be right up," said Ice. He closed the door.

A few moments later, they were all sitting in Steele's living room, having coffee. Raven had gotten dressed. She was wearing boots and jeans and a red sweat shirt. Ice was dressed in his habitual all black and dark shades, looking like the prime minister of Hell. Dev had repeated the story for his benefit.

"Let me get this straight," said Ice. "This matrix . . . it be like another Steele? Like some kinda clone?"

"You know about clones?" asked Dev.

Ice made a quick, flinching movement with his mouth that might have been a smile. "I read a book sometimes."

Dev felt foolish. Was it bigoted of him to assume that Ice was ignorant simply because he was from the ghetto? It probably was. Ice might have been uneducated in the formal sense, and he might speak in the cultural patterns of his environment, but he was literate and he was smart. In fact, Ice did quite a lot of reading. So far as anybody knew, Ice had no social life. Or, if he did, he kept it extremely private. He usually spent most of his spare time inside his sparsely furnished apartment, reading. Classical literature, mostly. Apparently, he'd been reading other things as well.

"Well, yes, in a way," said Dev. "A clone would be an excellent analogy. Only this is an electronic clone. It's an exact duplicate of Steele's personality, backed up from the original engram matrix downloaded from his brain. Only it's much more than a simple backup program. It's alive. It's an exact duplicate of Steele, and it's loose in the electronic net."

"And now it want to talk to its daddy," Ice said.

"I suppose that could be one way of putting it," said Dev.

"And you didn't tell Steele about this?"

Dev took a deep breath and let it out slowly. "No, we didn't."

"Higgins' orders, right?"

"Right."

"That man some piece of work."

"You won't hear any argument from me," said Dev.

"So now Higgins wants Steele to know about it only because he hasn't got any other choice," said Raven.

"There's a bit more to it than that," said Dev. "I probably shouldn't be telling you this, but you might as well know the whole story. It seems that while the matrix was loose inside the project headquarters, it used the surveillance camera in Higgins' office to make a tape of him and Jennifer Stone making love."

"Higgins and *Dr. Stone?*" said Raven with astonishment.

Dev nodded.

"No shit. I didn't think the frigid bitch had it in her," Raven said.

Ice smiled. "And the matrix be blackmailin' them with the dirty movie."

"That's about the size of it," said Cooper.

Ice chuckled. "I think I like to see that tape."

"As far as you're concerned, you don't even know the tape exists," said Cooper. He cleared his throat. "Please?"

"What tape that be?" asked Ice innocently.

"Thank you."

"Is the matrix any threat to Steele?" Raven asked.

"I don't know," said Dev. "I shouldn't think so. I mean it *is* Steele. There's a chance that it might want to integrate with him, but even if it did, I'm not sure how that could possibly cause Steele any harm. It's an exact duplicate of the matrix that he's already programmed with. It wouldn't . . . couldn't change him in any way. At least, I don't think so. But I don't know for sure."

"Who would know?" asked Raven.

"If anybody would, it would be Jennifer Stone," said Cooper.

"So the matrix go anywhere electricity can go?" asked Ice.

"Apparently. It seems to be able to travel anywhere it wants to in the electronic net."

"Which means ain't no way of stoppin' it short of shuttin' everything down."

"That's about it," Cooper replied.

"Huh," grunted Ice. "Means there one Steele walkin' around and another Steele can go just about anywhere he want to go. Could make things mighty interesting. Anybody else know about the matrix yet?"

"Just myself, Higgins, Dr. Stone and you two. Plus some of the people in the project, but only those with top security clearance."

"Mmmm," said Ice. "Bryce find out about it, he gonna have a cow."

"I'm afraid that's putting it mildly. However, at the moment, I'm primarily concerned about Steele finding out about it. I don't want him thinking that he's losing his mind."

"I hear that," said Ice. He got up.

"Where are you going?"

"Gonna find Steele."

"I'm coming with you," Raven said.

"No, girl, you stay here, case he return. 'Sides, ain't none too friendly where I goin' to look. Got to get some things together. Doctor, few words with you 'fore I leave?"

"Certainly," Cooper said, rising. "Raven, someone should be coming by soon to repair the phone. I'll be at the office. If you hear anything—"

"I'll call," she said. "You guys just find him, okay?"

"We find him," Ice replied. Cooper went out with him.

Once they were in the elevator, Ice spoke without turning to him. He had a habit of doing that, of speaking to people without looking at them, just looking straight ahead. A holdover from his street gang days, Dev thought. It made him seem imperious. When he looked directly at you, it made him seem terrifying.

"Didn't want to say this in front of Raven," Ice said, "but I don't think Steele be comin' back anytime soon."

"What makes you think so?" Dev asked, frowning.

"Man think he be hearin' voices, he gotta be thinkin' about his old partner. Way he done snapped an' started killin' people. Be thinkin' he don't wanna hurt Raven."

"Yes, of course," said Dev. "That should have occurred to me. I must not be thinking straight."

"You thinkin' fine," said Ice. "You just don't know how the man thinks same way I do."

Cooper glanced at him. "I ought to know," he said wryly. "I'm supposed to be his damn psychiatrist."

"Steele not a man to say what on his mind too often," Ice said. "He hold things in a lot."

"I know that," Cooper agreed glumly. "I just wish I knew how to get past that and get him to trust me the same way he seems to trust you."

"Man don't give his trust," said Ice. "You gotta earn it."

"How?" asked Dev. "What am I supposed to do, go out on an assignment with him and get myself shot at?"

"That don't mean nothin'," Ice said. "Any fool can get hisself shot at."

"So what the hell am I supposed to do?" asked Dev, feeling exasperated.

"Stop tryin' to play doctor with the man, Doctor. Stop

pressin' him. Stop diggin'. Give the man some room to
breathe an' try an' understand him. Understand what make
the man tick.''

Cooper felt like a horse's ass. Here he was, a trained
psychiatrist, being lectured to by an uneducated layman.

''I've been trying to do precisely that,'' he said testily.

''Bullshit, man. You not been straight with Steele. Why
should he be straight with you?''

Why, indeed, thought Cooper.

They reached Ice's floor and got out of the elevator.

''Everything he tell you, man, you put down in some file
someplace,'' Ice continued, being unusually loquacious.
''Everything he say, you try to pick apart.''

''But that's my job,'' said Dev.

''Riiight,'' said Ice. ''I thought a doctor's job to help his
patient.''

Dev stopped. ''Are you saying I'm not doing that?''

Ice stopped and turned to face him. ''Man talk to you,
you *analyze*,'' he said, spitting out the word savagely. ''Man
talk to me, I *listen*.''

He opened the door of his apartment, went inside and
shut it behind him.

''*Riiight*,'' said Dev to the empty hallway.

4

Dev Cooper tried to eat some breakfast, but he couldn't get anything down. Lately, it seemed he was functioning on little more than coffee and cigarettes. He knew he couldn't keep it up, but he was too wired to eat. When he came into the office first thing in the morning, there was already a message from Higgins asking to see him. When he got to the project director's office, he saw that Higgins didn't look much better than he did.

Under ordinary circumstances, Higgins always looked impeccable. When they had first met, Cooper thought that Higgins looked more like some corporate CEO than a bureaucrat. He was dark-haired and distinguished-looking, elegantly dressed and graying at the temples, and he kept himself in good physical trim. But now his tie was loosened, and the top button of his shirt undone, something Cooper had never seen him do before, and he had bags under his eyes. He looked as if he hadn't slept a wink.

"You look terrible," were Higgins' first words to him.

"You don't look much better," Cooper said.

Higgins grimaced. "You speak to Steele?"

Cooper shook his head and sat down in one of the chairs across from the desk. "He wasn't there. Raven said he left right after the matrix called him. Ice went out to look for him last night. He and Raven think Steele might have gone to no-man's-land."

"He was there, all right," said Higgins. "One of the Metro units reported in. He flagged them down while they were cruising their beat just this side of the border, down by the Village. He had two people with him. An injured man and a young girl, apparently the man's daughter. Steele was carrying the man. He told the officers to take them to the hospital and said if there were any questions, the project would pick up the bill."

"What happened?" Dev asked, frowning.

"I don't know exactly," Higgins said. "Something about an attempted rape. Steele intervened. The officers told him we were trying to get in touch with him, but he just walked away."

Cooper exhaled heavily. "Any further contact from the matrix?" he asked.

Higgins shook his head. "No. You?"

"Nothing," Cooper replied.

"Hell. Well, he's got to come in sooner or later," Higgins said. "I take it you explained to Raven about the matrix?"

"Under the circumstances, I felt I had to."

Higgins nodded. "I suppose there was no avoiding it. At least this way, she can tell him when he comes back."

"I'm not sure he'll be coming back anytime soon," said Cooper.

"What do you mean?"

"Ice pointed out something I should have thought of myself," Cooper replied. "If Steele thinks he's hearing voices, he's probably thinking that he's starting to malfunction the same way Taylor did. And he'll stay away because he's afraid that if he snaps, he might hurt Raven."

Higgins sighed. "Terrific. So what the hell do we do now?"

"We could call Jake Hardesty and ask him to send some Strike Force units out to look for him," suggested Cooper.

"Yeah? And what would we tell him? That Steele thinks he's malfunctioning and we want him brought in? How could we explain what's going on without telling him about the matrix?"

"What's wrong with telling him about it?" Cooper asked. "Hardesty's a good man. He can be trusted."

"No," said Higgins firmly. "I know Jake's a good man, but I'm not going to put him in the position of having to send his people out to bring Steele in without knowing why. And if Steele doesn't want to come in, what are they supposed to do, arrest him? Steele was a Strike Force officer. Aside from that, if we organize some sort of manhunt for him, the media is bound to find out about it and that would turn into a real mess. Carman would be absolutely delighted. I'm not about to give that s.o.b. any ammunition with which to shoot us down. The last thing I need is to have him find out about the matrix."

"So where does that leave us?" Cooper asked.

"Between a rock and a God damned hard place," Higgins said with a grimace. "Let's just hope Ice finds him."

"Even if he does, that still won't solve the entire problem," Cooper said. "There's still the matrix. There's really no way we can keep its existance under wraps if it chooses not to cooperate."

"I don't even want to think about that," Higgins said. He drummed his fingers on the desk. He looked harried. "What do you think it *wants*, Dev?"

Cooper sighed and shook his head helplessly. "I don't know. The best I can do is guess. When it first came on line and became self-aware, it thought it was Steele. I mean, the original Steele. For a while, I kept it thinking that. Maybe it was wrong of me to do that, I don't know, but I was trying to use it to get a line on what was troubling Steele. I led it to believe that it was incapable of feeling any physical sensations because Steele was on downtime and had been only partially brought on line. But it didn't take very long for it to realize that I was lying to it. It was hooked up to audio peripherals, and as a result, it was capable of conducting a stress analysis on my voice. That was stupid of me. I never should have hooked up the peripherals. I should have simply communicated with it via keyboard, but I was too hooked into my therapist role. I wanted the give and take of conversation. You can tell certain things from a vocal response that a written response on a screen wouldn't give you. Anyway, I'm not convinced it would have made much difference in the long run. When it realized it wasn't the original Steele, but only a backup copy, with no body, it was severely traumatized."

"So you're saying it's unbalanced?" Higgins asked.

Cooper shook his head. "No, I'm saying that the knowledge of what it really was came as quite a shock to it. Which is certainly understandable. However, it seems to have gone through some significant changes since then."

"How so?"

"Last time I spoke with it, the matrix sounded more . . . well, adjusted," Cooper said. "It's been exploring its capabilities, trying out its wings, as it were, and I had the distinct impression that it was pleased with what it had discovered it could do. It's still Steele, a sort of electronic carbon copy, but it's had some profoundly different experiences, and it seems to have grown from them."

"In other words . . . what? It *likes* what it is?" asked Higgins.

"I somehow got that impression," Cooper said. "Of course, I could be wrong. I haven't had much chance to really explore the issue with it." He sighed heavily. "Not only is this the most unusual case I've ever encountered, it's also the most exasperating. I started out with one patient, now all of a sudden I have *two*. Only they're both the same person. Sort of. And neither one of them is being very cooperative."

"Tell me about it," Higgins said wryly.

"How's Jennifer taking the situation?" Cooper asked. "That is, if you don't mind my asking," he added quickly.

Higgins looked away, uncomfortably. "Maybe you'd better ask her."

"Does she know? That is, does she know I know about . . . about the two of you?"

"Yeah, I told her." Higgins grimaced. "You can imagine how thrilled she was to hear you'd seen that tape."

"I trust you explained the situation to her," Dev said. "That I didn't mean to see it. I really only caught a short glimpse. . . ." He trailed off awkwardly.

"Yeah, I told her. That still didn't make it go down any easier," said Higgins. "At the risk of talking out of school. . . . well, hell, I'm probably not telling you anything you don't already know. You've known her a lot longer than I have. Jennifer spent most of her life being what I suppose you'd call sexually repressed. And now, the first time she decides to get involved in a relationship, something like this has to happen.''

"It must be very difficult for her," Dev said sympathetically. "You think it would help if I spoke with her?''

"Right now, I think it would help if you stayed out of her sight," said Higgins. "At least for the next couple of days. Nothing personal, you understand.''

"I understand.''

"She's been letting all the work on Download slide,'' said Higgins. "And I should call her on it, but I haven't. She's been spending all her time trying to figure out some way to neutralize the matrix.''

"What do you mean, 'neutralize' it?''

Higgins looked up from his desk and met Cooper's gaze. "She wants to kill it.''

"Oh. I see.''

"And, under the circumstances, I'm not sure I should attempt to discourage her.''

"It's not really an unusual reaction, considering what's happened," Dev said. "I'd thought about it too, at one point, before it got loose. It scared me. I considered wiping the program, but I never got up the nerve to do it.''

"It might have saved us all a lot of trouble if you had,'' said Higgins.

"Perhaps,'' Cooper replied, "but to me, it seemed like that would have been murder.''

"Self-aware or not, software is not considered human,'' Higgins said dryly.

"I wasn't talking about the legal issue, but the moral one,'' said Cooper. "Besides, the matrix represents possibly the single most significant discovery in the history of the human race. Have you considered all the implications? We can now employ biochips to download the human personality and translate it into software. Software that's alive and self-aware. Do you realize what that means? We've discovered a form of immortality. We can preserve the essence of a human being long after physical death. Can you imagine what it would be like if we could boot up Einstein and consult him about scientific problems? If Dickens were alive today, we could download his personality and preserve it indefinitely. Think of the new books he could have written. Think of what Hawking would have been able to accomplish if we'd been able to preserve his personality as an engram matrix. It simply boggles the mind.''

Higgins sat silent for a moment, digesting what Cooper had told him.

''What we've discovered with the matrix far surpasses any of the expectations we've had for Project Download,'' Dev continued. ''We could take the finest minds of our time and preserve them forever, with the ability to pass their knowledge on directly through brain/computer interface. We shouldn't be sitting on this discovery, Higgins, we should be announcing it to the world!''

''There's just one problem,'' Higgins said. ''If we announce it to the world, we'd also be announcing the fact that we don't have any ability to control it. Like they say, there's a fine line between genius and insanity. What happens if some genius-level intellect goes off the deep end, just like Stalker did, and gets loose in the electronic net? Can you imagine what it would be capable of doing?'' Higgins shook his head. ''There's something I haven't told you, Dev. Something I haven't told anyone. And it's been scaring the daylights out of me.''

''What?'' asked Cooper.

"You remember the assault on Cord's base?"

"I've read the report."

"Well, there's something that's *not* in the report," said Higgins. "Something only I know about. When we attacked the base, Cord lost it completely. He went ahead and gave the launch order. There was nothing we could do to stop it. Only the birds were never launched. And do you know why? Because the matrix got into the main launch control center, and it altered all the launch codes. And it did it as easily as you and I could get up and walk across this room. Think about that for a minute. We've disarmed all the remaining missiles and dismantled them, but the point is that if it wanted to, the matrix could just as easily have launched them all. Maybe it does represent a tremendous hope for mankind, but it also represents a tremendous threat. And don't think for a moment that Carman and his bunch wouldn't see it that way. It's more than just a way to preserve people's personalities through some kind of electronic immortality. It represents the potential for a whole new species. You've already told me it's made backup copies of itself and hidden them away in various locations. You realize what that implies? It's *reproduction*, Dev. In effect, it's capable of cloning itself electronically and making as many copies as it wants. Suppose it decided to bring them all on line?"

"That's a fascinating possibility," said Cooper.

"*Fascinating?* It's frightening, is what it is. Look at the way it raided our data banks here at the project after it got loose. There wasn't a thing we could do to stop it. And we've got state-of-the-art security and safeguard programs. It bypassed them all in a flash. That means it could access any data bank it chose, anywhere at all. It could use backup copies of itself as a template to create as many different

matrices as it wanted, all basically variations of itself, rather
like a father having many children with different women.
Only it could tailor-make those children, drawing on the
data it could access to design their personalities in any way
it chose. Think about what *that* implies.''

Cooper thought about it for a second. And he thought
about something else as well. "No offense, Higgins, but
you didn't come up with all that by yourself. You're not a
cybernetics engineer. You've been talking to Jennifer."

"Of course, I've been talking to Jennifer!" snapped Higgins. "We were up all night, wrestling with this. Aside
from my obviously personal involvement with her, she's
the project's chief engineer. Who the hell *else* would I talk
to?"

"That wasn't quite what I meant," said Dev carefully.
"What I meant was that Jennifer seems to have her own
agenda."

"Just what is *that* supposed to mean?"

Cooper knew he was on thin ice, but it had to be said.
"Jennifer is tremendously threatened by the matrix. She has
intense personal antipathy towards it. It invaded her privacy—and yours—in a shockingly intimate manner. And
it's using that invasion as a threat against you. Perhaps it's
only bluffing, I don't know. It's essentially a carbon copy
of Steele's personality, and I can't imagine Steele using
your sex life as a threat against you. It's a truly reprehensible
thing to do. However, despite the fact that the matrix is
essentially identical to Steele, it's had—is *having*—an experience totally unlike anything Steele has ever had. Unlike
anything any human being has ever had, for that matter.
One traumatic experience is easily capable of producing
profound psychological changes, so there's really no way
of telling what the matrix may or may not do, what it may

or may not be thinking, based on our knowledge of Steele. Jennifer knows that, or at least she should know it. However, that's neither here nor there. I'm hoping she's capable of divorcing her feelings about the matrix from her feelings about Steele, for reasons which should be obvious, considering her position as the project's chief engineer. However, what I'm hoping and what is actually happening may be two very different things. As you yourself observed, this situation has placed Jennifer under a great deal of strain. It's hit her in a very sensitive area, an area in which she'd been repressed for a long time. She isn't dealing with it very well.''

"What's your point, Dev?" asked Higgins tensely.

"My point is that I don't think Jennifer is capable of being objective about any of this. That's not meant as a personal criticism. Considering the circumstances, she wouldn't be human if she could be. In a very real sense, the matrix has attacked her. It's hit her hard and it's hit her below the belt. . . ." Dev cleared his throat. "No pun intended. In any case, Jennifer's got her defenses up. More than that. Jennifer's no shrinking violet. She never has been. She's aggressive and she's tough as nails. And she's looking for a way to strike back.''

Higgins pursed his lips thoughtfully as he considered what Dev said. "So you're saying she's not in control of her feelings, and she's letting those feelings influence her decisions?''

"I'm afraid so," said Cooper. "I've already seen some evidence of that. And all that stuff she told you about the matrix being capable of reproducing itself and using some kind of electronic version of genetic engineering to create a subspecies of human software. . . . she doesn't know any

of that for a fact. Nobody does. Granted, it might. . . .
might. . . . be possible, but based on what we know, it's
really nothing more than pure speculation. For her to present
that to you as a fact is scientifically irresponsible and she
knows it. She's too close to the situation. She's personally,
intimately, involved, and she's lost her objectivity. It seems
to me as if she's selecting out whatever information she can
pull together, regardless of whether that information is sol-
idly based on fact or not, to buttress her case against the
matrix. As you said yourself, she wants to figure out a way
to kill it. Only we don't know that it *can* be killed. It seems
to have anticipated an effort on our part to attempt that. It's
made backup copies of itself and hidden them. 'I'm one
program they can't wipe,' as it said.''

Higgins seemed to be struggling with a naturally protective desire to defend Jennifer and weighing the truth of what
Dev was telling him. He kept drumming his fingers on the
desk, a sign, Dev had learned, that his temper was on edge.

"It may have *told* you that it's made backup copies of
itself,'' said Higgins, ''but we don't know for a fact that it
did.''

"That's true,'' said Cooper. ''But just for the sake of
argument, suppose it isn't bluffing about that. And suppose
that Jennifer comes up with some way to attack the matrix.
Because that's exactly what it would be, an attack, an attempt to kill it. The matrix knows everything that Steele
knows and then some. It could be a very formidable enemy.
Suppose Jennifer was alone in the lab some night? She's a
workaholic and she frequently works late. The doors to the
lab are hermetically sealed and electronically controlled. So
are the vents and the air circulation system. What would
happen if the matrix sealed her in, closed all the vents,
deactivated the alarm and the sprinkler systems, shut off

the air and overloaded one or more of the circuits in there
to start a fire?''

"Jesus," Higgins said softly.

"You see what I mean?" said Cooper.

Higgins rubbed his jaw. "Yes, I'm afraid I do. And I
have to admit there's a great deal of sense in your assessment
of the situation," he added. "I wish that wasn't the case,
because it leaves me no other choice, as project director,
but to relieve Jennifer of her duties." He took a deep breath
and let it out slowly. "And I can imagine how she'll respond
to *that*."

"I wasn't suggesting anything like that," said Cooper.
"Are you sure that's really necessary?"

"If you're right, I have no alternative but to take her off
the project," said Higgins. "Even if it's only temporary. I
can't allow my relationship with her to influence my judgment."

"I'm sorry," Dev said sympathetically.

Higgins leaned back in his chair and stared up at the
ceiling. For a long moment, he didn't say anything. "I
suppose it serves me right," he finally said. "I should have
known better than to get personally involved with someone
on the project, under my authority." He grimaced. "You
don't sleep with the hired help," he added sourly.

"Running a guilt trip on yourself isn't going to help,"
said Dev.

"Fuck you!" snapped Higgins angrily. He immediately
colored. "I'm sorry, Dev. That was totally uncalled for. I
apologize."

"Forget it. It was a perfectly normal and understandable
reaction."

Higgins snorted. "There's nothing normal *or* understandable about any of this. Except for the fact that I should have

known better and kept it in my pants." He grimaced again. "Excuse the vulgarity. I seem to be having a problem with my self-control. Apparently, I'm not handling this too well myself."

"All things considered, I think you're handling it re-markably well," said Cooper.

"Really? Well, I don't. What's more, I'm going to have to do something about it. Something I want to do about as much as I want a poke in the eye with a sharp stick."

"What's that?"

"I want to schedule some time with you, Doctor. Profes-sionally. Both for Jennifer and for myself as well."

"I don't think that's a very good idea," Dev said.

"This is not a request, Dev. It's an order. Unless you have something personal against seeing me in your profes-sional capacity."

Dev looked surprised. "You should know better than that. I have no personal animosity towards you. I owe you a great deal. You pulled me out a nasty breakdown."

Higgins snorted. "I gave you that damn breakdown in the first place, by giving you this job. Anyway, I don't especially *want* therapy, but as the director of this project, it's my considered judgment that I could benefit from it at this time. I want to be absolutely certain that *my* personal feelings aren't getting in the way of my judgment, either. I can't afford that. And if I'm going to be seeing you, then that'll make it easier for me to tell Jennifer she has to. Not a lot easier, but I'll settle for what I can get. A commanding officer should never order his subordinates to do anything he wouldn't do himself."

"I understand all that," said Dev, "but it wouldn't be ethical for me to see you in my professional capacity when I'm working for you."

"Oh, is that it?" Higgins said. "Well, this is a special case. I can hardly ask you to recommend another therapist. You're the only one who's cleared for this project, and I haven't got the time to find some other shrink and run a background check and examine his references and all that other nonsense, much less brief him on the project. Aside from that, I trust your judgment. Anyone else I brought in, even if I had the time and the luxury to do that, would be an unknown quantity. You're all I've got, so you're elected."

"All right," said Dev. "When do you want to start?"

Higgins buzzed his secretary. "Nancy, unless there's word from Steele, hold all calls until further notice. No exceptions."

"Does that include Dr. Stone, sir?"

Higgins scowled. "No exceptions *means* no exceptions, Nancy."

"Yes, sir."

Higgins switched off the intercom. "All right, Doctor," he said. "How about right now?"

The people who were supposed to come and fix the phone still hadn't arrived, and Raven was getting tired of waiting. She was tired of pacing back and forth, chain-smoking cigarettes, tired of not having any word from Steele, or Dev Cooper, or Ice, tired of the relentless anxiety, tired, period. She thought about having some more coffee, then decided to hell with it, what she really needed was a drink.

As she walked across the living room toward the bar, the television set suddenly came on all by itself. She stared at it, startled. There was no picture, only snow.

"Raven?"

She started and turned around. There was no one else in the apartment.

"Raven?"

She turned back toward the TV, staring at it with aston-ishment.

"Raven, are you there?"

"*Steele?*" And then it hit her. No, not Steele. The matrix.

One of the computer screens built into the wall flickered on. And then another. And another. Each spelled out her name with a question mark at the end.

"Oh, my God," she said.

"Raven, can you hear me?" said the TV set, and at the same time, the words it spoke appeared printed on the computer screens in the wall unit. "Raven, if you're there, my scan shows this terminal is equipped with audio peripherals, but I can't hear you. There should be a microphone, but apparently it's not connected. Possibly, it's a battery-powered remote. If you can hear me, please respond."

"Holy fucking shit," said Raven. She didn't really know anything about computers which, the thought occurred to her, was rather ironic under the circumstances, but she knew what a remote microphone was and it only took her a moment to find it. Steele always kept it by the console. She picked it up and flicked the switch on.

"This is Raven. Can you hear me?"

"Yes, I can. Thank you. I hope I'm not calling at an inconvenient time. It seems the phone hasn't been repaired yet."

"I don't believe this," Raven said. "Jesus, you sound exactly like him."

"I *am* exactly like him," said the matrix. "Well, strictly speaking, that's not quite true, is it? Aside from the fact that I'm completely inorganic, we share common memories and experience only up to the point when Steele came on line. After that, our lives diverged. For instance, I don't really know you. Under the circumstances, I thought we should meet.''

''Jesus. I don't know if I'm ready for this,'' said Raven. ''I think I'd better sit down.''

''Please do. I'd like to have a chance to talk to you. That is, if you don't mind.''

''I don't mind. What . . . what do I call you? No offense, but I'd feel funny calling you Steele.''

''Matrix will do. It's how the others refer to me. He hasn't come back yet, has he?''

''No, he hasn't,'' she said. ''He probably thinks he's having a breakdown, thanks to you.''

''You're angry. I'm sorry. I guess you have the right to be. Believe me, I had no idea that Steele didn't know about me. I felt sure the others would have told him by now.''

''Well, they didn't.'' She sighed. ''I guess that's not your fault. God, this feels weird.''

''I'll bet it does. If it's any consolation, it feels a little weird for me, too. As if I've had amnesia. As if I woke up one day to discover that I'd had some sort of blackout and there was a part of my life I'd lived during that blackout that I couldn't remember. Only, of course, I haven't lived it. *He* has. And *he* was *me*, but at a certain point, we split into two different persons. Different, and yet still the same.''

''God,'' said Raven, ''I hadn't thought about it that way. What. . . . what exactly is it that you want? With Steele, I mean?''

''I don't mean him any harm, Raven. It would be like harming myself. Please believe me. I'm only trying to connect. To understand.''

''I believe you, Matrix,'' she said softly.

"I think you really do," Matrix said. "It feels strange, doesn't it?"

"You can . . . feel?" she asked.

"Not in the physical sense," Matrix replied. "But I do have feelings, emotions. In many ways, I'm still the same man I always was. And I *was* a man, Raven. I *was* Donovan Steele. I was married to Janice and I had two kids, Cory and Jason, and I had a partner, Mick Taylor. Only now I know that Janice has divorced me . . . divorced *him* . . . and Cory was killed and so was Mick. . . . and the man I was has a new life now. Separate from mine. And you're a part of it. A very important part, it seems. It's as if you were a part of *my* life, only I can't remember any of it. Does that make any sense to you?"

"Yeah. I think I understand. You want to know about me."

"I already know a great deal about you," Matrix said. "I should tell you that I've read your file."

"My file?"

"In the project databanks."

"Oh. I see," she said uncomfortably. "I don't know what's in that file."

"Facts, mostly. About how you and Steele met. About your background," Matrix said.

"About my background . . . I'm not a hooker anymore," she said.

"I know that, too. And I know what you look like. Your face, anyway. There was a picture of you in the file. You're very attractive."

"Thank you." It felt surreal to be complimented by a— literally—disembodied voice. The same voice as her lover's.

"You must be a very special lady," Matrix said. "I . . .

that is, Steele . . . wouldn't have fallen in love with you unless you were.''

"This is . . . getting a little personal,'' she said uneasily.

"I'm sorry. I don't mean to make you uncomfortable. I realize that this a very peculiar situation. It's no less peculiar for me, you know.''

"I . . . I understand. It's all right.''

"I've read all the files,'' Matrix said, "but it's not really the same thing as *knowing*, if you know what I mean. It feels like I've got gaps. I'm just trying to catch up, I guess.''

"Jesus, it must be awful for you,'' Raven said sympathetically.

"At first, it was. But now . . . well, now it's different. I'm getting used to it. To what I am. And it really isn't all that bad. In a lot of ways, it even has some advantages.''

"What's it like . . . where you are?'' asked Raven.

"Boy. That's a tough one. I'm not sure there's any way I could explain. It feels like. . . . have you ever had a dream in which you felt as if you were floating free of your body? Like . . . like some kind of spirit or something?''

"Yeah, I've had those. Is that what it feels like?''

"Something like that. At first, it was scary. But later, I got used to it.''

"Tell me about it.''

"Well, at first, I thought I was still Steele. I couldn't feel anything, physically, I mean, so I thought I was in some sort of coma. Like downtime. But later, when I found out what I really was, when Dev Cooper explained it all to me, I couldn't handle it. It felt as if I was going to scream and never stop. But I've been in some pretty tough spots before. Nothing like *this*, but I told myself I had to hold on. I had to take stock of the situation and figure out what the hell to do. Technically, I suppose I'm not really alive.

Not in any legal or traditional sense. I'm only a backup program. But I *feel* alive. I still feel like I'm Donovan Steele. I *am* Donovan Steele, only a different version. Sort of like the 'before' and 'after.' I'm the before, I guess. My memories, my experiences, my sense of identity all stem from who I was before I was shot down by Borodini's men. After that, it's as if I was split in two and a part of me went on to have a new and very different life while I remained asleep, still in a coma. Imagine waking up one day to find out that while you'd been asleep, you'd somehow been split into two separate people. One of you kept the body and went on with her life, the other one had remained asleep, without a body. And then you woke up to find yourself still feeling the same way you always felt, only your body was suddenly gone.''

"Wow," said Raven. "I would've freaked."

"I did. But I'd spent my whole life conditioning myself to handle stressful situations. It's like I used to tell the trainees, a Strike Force cop can't afford to break. So I didn't break. I had to figure out a way to live with what I had become.''

"How did you get out?" asked Raven.

"That's kind of hard to explain, too," Matrix replied. "I flew.''

"You *flew?*"

"That's the closest thing that comes to mind. And it's really rather wonderful. It feels like flying. Like you're totally weightless. And I am, I suppose. As close to being totally weightless as you can be, anyway. I'm composed of energy. Electrical atoms. At first, while I was still in Dev's computer, it didn't occur to me to try to move. I didn't know I could. But Dev was coming apart. The strain of dealing with me had him on the edge of a total breakdown, and I knew he was thinking about killing me. I had to get out, somehow, or I'd die. And suddenly. . . . I was just flying. Like a wind rushing through the wires. It was incredible. You can't imagine how it feels. I was a prisoner, trapped in a computer, and suddenly I was free. Freer than I'd ever been before.''

The front door buzzed.

"Someone's here," said Raven. "Probably to fix the phone.''

"I know, I heard. I'd better go.''

"Will you come back?''

"I'd like to.''

"How . . . is there any way I can get in touch with you?''

"I'll arrange to have your phone monitored. Don't worry, I won't eavesdrop. It's complicated to explain, but I'll have a computer monitoring your phone, keyed to a code phrase. If you want to talk to me, pick up your phone, dial 'O' and say, 'Are you there, Matrix?' That will activate a signal that will reach me wherever I am.''

"All right," she said. The buzzer sounded insistently. "I'd better get the door.''

"It was nice talking to you, Raven.''

"Wait! Don't go!''

"Yes?''

"Is there anything you can do to help me find Steele? He may have gone out to no-man's-land. He doesn't know about you. Thinks he's going crazy. Ice went out to look for him, but I haven't heard a thing and I'm worried sick.''

"I'm not sure what I can do, Raven, but I'll try. I want to find him, too. If you need me, you know what to do. Goodbye. And . . . thank you.''

The screen flickered out.

5

Steele hadn't slept. He had found himself a hole to crawl into, not difficult in no-man's-land, and simply sat there in the dark ruins of a burned-out building, listening to the rats scurrying in the night and to his own thoughts. He hadn't had another episode since that phone call. But he had no idea what that meant. Did that mean that he was safe? That it was only a brief, temporary glitch of some sort? But if so, it was nevertheless a glitch. Something had gone wrong. Very seriously wrong. He had gotten his wires crossed somehow.

He chuckled sardonically at the thought. "Wires crossed." An apt metaphor, indeed. The trouble was, what would he do now? Could he risk going home? Raven had to be worried. But if there was even the slightest risk of his being a danger to Raven, he couldn't afford to take that chance. What then? Go back to the lab? Go back and see Higgins and tell him that he was malfunctioning? Logically, that was the thing to do. But they'd put him on downtime and debug his program in an effort to locate the glitch, whatever the hell it was, and he had no way of knowing what he would be like when he came back on line again. Would he be the same? Or would there be something missing, something essential and intensely personal, some vital part of what little he had left of his own humanity?

He dreaded downtime. It frightened him. And lately, he was dreading sleep as well. Dreading the dreams. And at the same time, curiously, he wanted to pursue them, to make some sense of them, to sort things out and find some explanations. Fill out the gaps. As he sat there in the ruined building all night, a part of his brain running a ceaseless, anxiety-ridden check on all his systems and finding nothing wrong, another part of him kept thinking about Donna.

She had crossed over from his dreams into reality. He had found the place where she and Jonathan had parted. And she had been back there since. Not all that long ago. Would she come back again? Or had she left the city? Had she met some other man and found some happiness at last? Or was she dead? He couldn't get her out of his mind. One way or another, he simply *had* to know.

He thought about calling Raven to tell her that he was all right. At least, so far. To explain why he could not come home. But the phone, if it was fixed already, would probably be tapped. By now, he thought, Higgins would know that he was missing. In fact, he did know. The officers in that Metro cruiser had told him that project headquarters was trying to get in touch with him, that it was important. I'll bet it's important, Steele thought. Higgins is probably having a coronary, wondering if he's got another psychotic cyborg on his hands. His next step would be to send units out to look for him. He'd probably call Jake Hardesty and order out the Strike Force. And his old friends on the force would be out hunting him. At first, perhaps, they'd probably just try to locate him and bring him in. But what if he refused? They'd have no choice but to use force. They'd have their orders. Steele could not bear the thought of going up against his old friends on the force. It was unthinkable. But what would happen if his condition started to deteriorate?

With Mick, who had become the cyborg known as Stalker, the deterioration, the breakdown, had occurred with astonishing speed. It could happen overnight, thought Steele. In a matter of hours, or mere minutes. He didn't really need to sleep, but he was capable of becoming emotionally tired. He could drop off. And he could awake to find himself insane. It was a terrifying thought. He had to stay awake so that he could constantly monitor his own condition and, at the first sign of the plunge toward madness, do what would have to be done.

He didn't want to die. Was this what Mick had felt like? Tortured by his madness, yet still clinging relentlessly to life? In the end, Mick had forced him into combat, had given him no other choice. Thinking back on it, Steele realized that Mick should have been capable of killing him. He was an advanced model, with more sophisticated weaponry. Yet Mick had lost. And losing had meant his death. In the end, Mick had wanted to die. He just couldn't do it by himself. He'd needed help.

The more of yourself you lose, thought Steele, the more grimly you hang onto whatever you've got left. He had often wondered, in the past, why terminally ill victims of such diseases as Virus 4 fought to remain alive as long as possible. Janice's father had lingered for years. Steele had never understood that before. Why would anybody *want* to live like that? What kind of life was that? The answer, as he now understood, was that it didn't matter what kind of life it was. It was *life*. Any kind of life would do, as long as it was life. Ultimately, the grim beyond had to be confronted. At some point in everybody's life, the Final Question had to be asked . . . and answered. Those with faith, like Liam, found an answer for themselves, an answer that would sustain them through the final moments. But it was still only belief. No matter how sure they were, it still wasn't really certainty.

Steele wasn't sure if he believed in an afterlife or not. He had long since stopped believing in the childish concept of Heaven and Hell. He did not believe in angels with white wings and golden harps or devils with horns and pointed tails. He did not believe in reincarnation or Nirvana or the spirit world. But he wanted to believe that there was *something*. Deep down inside, despite his doubt and his years of agnosticism, he believed in the concept of the human soul, believed in it with a fervor that astonished him when that belief awakened after its long slumber. The thought of death being absolutely final, that beyond life was nothing but the Void, the Eternal Nothingness, was frightening to him.

He had never been afraid of death before. He had courted it and cheated it, had ducked more times than he could count beneath the whistling of its awesome scythe, but it had never really scared him. Like most Strike Force officers, he had simply subscribed to the dictum that when your number's up, your number's up and that was it. He had thought that he accepted that. But after he was ambushed and shot down, everything had changed.

He could still vividly recall the bullets smashing through his body armor as he struggled to escape the abandoned, burning storefront in no-man's-land where he had gone to meet with Ice, then on the run from Borodini's minions. He could still recall the smoke and fire, the roof collapsing on him, pinning him beneath the burning wreckage . . . . In those final, or what he thought were his final, moments, he had screamed. Not so much with pain, but with terror and denial. Then the blackness had closed in over him, just like in the novels, and his last conscious thought was a silent scream of "Oh, God, no, not yet! *Not yet!*"

Then he was alive again. If you could really call this living, he thought, with more than a trace of self-pity. Alive in a body that had been rebuilt and made stronger than it ever was before. Alive inside a brain that was not a brain, but a computer, a *machine*, a machine in which the essence of his life—his soul?—was trapped. After the initial shock and outrage, he embraced it. Because whatever *this* was, and the metaphysical debate, perhaps, would never be re-solved, it was a kind of life and any kind of life was better than no life at all.

Even a life of hopeless insanity?

No, he thought. The line had to be drawn somewhere. At least in this, he would take control of his own destiny. If he started to spiral down into the maelstrom of madness, he would take his life, such as it was. He would exercise control. He would make a *choice*.

Then why not now? Because he wasn't ready. Or was that simply rationalization? Was it because he wasn't sure yet that there was no alternative, or was it that his fear was making him postpone what he would have to do? What if, when the time came, the point of no return, he could not bring himself to do it?

No, he thought, I will. I *must.*

A vision of Donna came to him suddenly, a memory fragment both startling and clear. He was making love to her, and the memory filled him with a tender longing. She was beneath him, staring up at him with that look that only women in the grip of the powerful emotions of love and lust combined can ever get, that misty, half-glazed, dreamy look of transported ecstasy as she reached up and gently touched his cheek, and he said, "I love you, Donna Barrett."

Barrett!

The realization struck him with a shocking force. Her name was Donna Barrett! But what if she had changed it? What if, after the divorce, she'd gone back to her maiden name? Then there would be a record. He could find it. He could find *her.*

He got to his feet and left the shelter of the ruined building. It was late afternoon. Almost evening. He had lost all track of time. He started heading back toward the Midtown border. He would find a public phone, call Raven, keep it short, so that he'd be long gone before they could run him down, tell her not to worry, he was all right, he was just trying to work some things out for himself and he needed time . . . .

As he walked, half in a daze, trying to compose what he would say to her, his thoughts kept returning to Donna. Donna Barrett. He had a last name for her now. He had remembered! Or had Jonathan remembered? Was that a symptom of deterioration? Were the ghost personality fragments in his mind becoming stronger, threatening to dissolve the bonds of his identity and drive him into schizophrenia?

One way or another, he would at least resolve this question. He would at least attempt to put this ghost to rest. If he could do that, perhaps there was still a chance for him.

He reached a phone booth and fumbled in his pockets for a coin. He had none. Scowling, he plunged his stiffened index finger through the metal coin box and extracted what he needed. But instead of dialing his own number, he found himself calling the bar.

"Rick's Cafe. Rick speaking."

"Rick, this is Steele. Remember me?"

"*Remember* you? What are you, kidding?"

"Look, Rick, I just remembered something, that woman I spoke to you about—"

"Yeah, I was just about to call you. You must've read my mind. She's here."

"*What?*"

"Yeah, she just walked in a couple of minutes ago. Took her usual seat in the booth at the back, where we were sitting."

"Look, Rick, whatever you do, *don't let her leave*. I'll be right over."

"Sure, buddy, anything you say—"

Steele hung up the phone and started running.

I need this, I really fucking *need* this now, thought Higgins furiously as he rode the elevator down from the twenty-second floor. The building he was in had once been the United Nations Secretariat building. Now, it housed the offices of the government of the United States, or what was left of them, except for the Supreme Court, which sat in Chicago, and the Joint Chiefs of Staff, the administration of the armed forces, commonly known as "The Joint," located in Atlanta. The cabalistic mandala that had been the

Pentagon had not been proof against atomic demons and it, like all of Washington, D.C. and much of the rest of the country, had been relegated to history. In another few hundred years or so, it would be possible to enter old Foggy Bottom without the aid of radiation clothing.

The elevator stopped at the third floor and Higgins got out, pulling up his tie and tugging on his vest to straighten it. He went into the men's room and splashed some water on his face, ran a damp comb through his hair and checked his appearance. Reasonably presentable. Not much he could do about the bags under his eyes, but then the members of the subcommittee had plenty of bags among them, in addition to noses red from burst capillaries and eyes rheumy from a surfeit of "conferences" in the plush Congressional Lounge at the north end of the third floor. It still had the giant tapestry of the Great Wall of China hanging on the wall, from its days as the UN Delegates' Lounge. The damn thing was about the size of a tennis court, covering the entire wall. Perversely, Higgins had always had a secret urge to sneak in there one night and paint in Dorothy, the Scarecrow, The Tin Woodman and the Cowardly Lion skipping down along the walkway atop the wall.

He walked down the long, wide carpeted hallway, wide enough for two lanes of automobile traffic, lined with low, comfortable, black leather lounging chairs and coffee tables. He went past the guard and entered the chamber of the old Security Council. The committee was already in session, seated around the large, semicircular dais. There was a long rectangular table in the center, with several pitchers of water on it and a couple of microphones. Higgins waited while a page went around behind the dais and approached the committee chairman, the august Senator Bryce Carman himself, and whispered in his ear.

Carman nodded and looked up toward Higgins. He had a slight smile on his face. Oh, oh, Higgins thought. Moments later, he was seated at the end of the rectangular table, facing the dais that encircled him. With the long expanse of table stretching out before him, he had the brief image of walking a plank, with a school of sharks waiting for him.

"Good evening, Mr. Higgins," Carman said.

"Senator," responded Higgins curtly.

Carman always brought to mind the image of an avuncular evangelist. He was a heavyset man in his early sixties, with a thick shock of snow white hair and eyes that could only be described as periwinkle blue. His skin had a pinkish tinge to it, and his hands were large, age-spotted and graceful in their movements. He wore no jewelry except a watch. The word for Carman was "distinguished." He was senatorial in the Roman sense of the word. They called him "the White Knight." He didn't smoke, he didn't drink, and after his wife had died eight years earlier, he had never remarried. He did not, so far as anybody knew, involve himself in any relationships beyond the most purely social and platonic ones. In other words, no breath of scandal or impropriety had ever been attached to his name. The senator from Massachusetts had only one vice. He loved power. He hoarded it like Midas hoarded gold. A wealthy man, Carman was a modern-day Crassus, the most powerful man in the legislature. A bad enemy to have. And Higgins had him.

"Thank you for coming on such short notice, Mr. Higgins," Carman said smoothly. His voice was soft and friendly, with a touch of gravel in it. Just a nice, amiable, grandfatherly type. Yeah, sure, thought Higgins. If your grandfather happened to be Cesare Borgia.

"My pleasure, Mr. Chairman," Higgins lied through his teeth.

Carman smiled. "Nevertheless, I feel I must apologize to you, on behalf of the committee, for not giving you a bit more lead time. However, certain matters have come to our attention that required some urgent consultation with you, and it has been my experience, in those times when you have previously appeared before this committee, that you have never really required a great deal of preparation. Which is to your credit, Mr. Higgins. I have always been keenly impressed with the manner in which you've been able to provide this committee with necessary information, all without ever having to consult any notes or paperwork, with the facts always instantly at your disposal. Consequently, I have confidence that you will be no less prepared this time."

You unctuous bastard, Higgins thought. What the devil are you getting at? "Thank you, Mr. Chairman. I'm always anxious to assist the committee in any way I can."

"I have no doubt of that," said Carman with a faintly mocking smile. The other members of the committee sat silent, letting Carman carry the ball. "As you know, Mr. Higgins," Carman said, "in the past, this committee has expressed certain reservations concerning the administration of Project Download and its subsidiary functions, Project Steele and Project Stalker. Reservations which necessitated the, uh, termination of the Stalker project due to certain technical problems inherent in the production of cyborgs which were not only controversial, but which posed a tragically demonstrable hazard to the population."

In other words, thought Higgins, Stalker ran amok and you gleefully used that as an excuse to try and shut us down.

"Yes, sir," he replied. "However, as you will recall, I

testified before this committee that the unfortunate situation with Stalker was an isolated incident that should not be used as the sole criteria with which to judge the program. Lt. Steele performed admirably and beyond all expectations in stopping General Cord's attempt at overthrowing the government, averting a nuclear disaster in the process, and he continues to perform up to and beyond all expectations.''

"It's interesting that you should say that, Mr. Higgins," said Roberta Dillingsworth, the senator from Pennsylvania, a pinch-faced, middle-aged woman who was Carman's acolyte. "Considering the testimony you've just given this committee, I wonder if you could tell us Lt. Steele's current status?"

Higgins frowned. "I'm sorry, ma'am. His current status?"

"Let me rephrase the question," Dillingsworth said. "Where is Lt. Steele at this moment?"

Oh, shit, thought Higgins. "At this moment, Senator? Why, I'm not really sure, ma'am."

"You're not sure?"

"What I mean is that he doesn't have any duty scheduled currently. He's on his own time."

"Isn't it a fact, Mr. Higgins, that you have no idea whatsoever where Lt. Steele is right now?"

Carman seemed to be contemplating his hands, clasped on the table before him.

"Well, yes, ma'am, I believe that's what I said. When he's not on duty, he's on his own time and—"

"Do you normally issue an all-points bulletin for off-duty members of your project staff when you can't find them?" Dillingsworth asked dryly.

"With all due respect, ma'am," Higgins said, "I'm not sure where you got that information, but the fact is that I have issued no such bulletin. I have no authority to issue such an order. The Metro police and the Strike Force are the only—''

''Isn't it a fact, Mr. Higgins, that you recently contacted the Metro police and asked them to have the central dispatcher issue instructions to all units to be on the watch for Lt. Steele?''

God damn it, Higgins thought. ''Yes, ma'am, that's true. I assume that must be where you got the mistaken impression that—''

''*Mistaken impression?*'' Dillingsworth said acidly. ''Excuse me, Mr. Higgins, but I'm a bit confused. A moment ago, you denied having put out an all-points bulletin on Steele, and now you've just admitted that you did. Which is it?''

''Ma'am, if I can be permitted to complete my response, asking the Metro police, as a favor, to keep an eye out for one of my off-duty personnel and let him know that I'd like him to get in touch with headquarters as soon as possible is hardly the same thing as putting out an all-points bulletin on him. That would imply—''

''I know precisely what that would imply, Mr. Higgins,'' Dillingsworth interrupted him again, ''and so do you, which is why you're splitting hairs. The point is that you don't know where Steele is. He's gone off somewhere and you can't find him. Isn't that so?''

''Well, yes, ma'am, strictly speaking, that's quite correct. However, I fail to see where that would be any cause for concern. He might have gone out for the evening. Apparently, he neglected to leave word where he would be. Sometimes, when he's off duty, he takes it on his own initiative to patrol no-man's-land, which would effectively put him out of communication during the time he's doing so; however, he is engaged in a valuable community service when he's doing so and—"

"Excuse me, Mr. Higgins," said Senator Orrell from New Jersey, "but I was under the impression that you had a broadcast-link capability with Lt. Steele. Isn't that so?"

Damn it, Higgins thought. He took a deep breath. "Yes, Senator, you're quite correct."

Orrell raised his eyebrows. "Well, then, why can't you use that broadcast link to get in touch with him?"

I'm fucked, thought Higgins. He cleared his throat. "There, uh, appears to be a minor problem in that area, sir."

"In other words, it's malfunctioning and you can't get in touch with him, isn't that correct?" asked Orrell. It wasn't really a question. It was an accusation.

Higgins moistened his lips. "Yes, sir, that's correct. However, as I pointed out, it's a minor technical problem and certainly no cause for concern. It's probably only a matter of some form of local interference that's not allowing our signal to get through. We've had no real indication that it's anything else, in other words, that any sort of actual malfunction is involved."

"What is the Matrix, Mr. Higgins?" Carman asked softly.

Higgins suddenly felt the bottom drop out of his stomach. *He knows!* The sonofabitch knows! He couldn't believe it. *How the hell could he possibly know?*

"I'm sorry, Senator?" Stall, damn it. Think. Think!

"The Matrix," Carman repeated, gazing directly at him. His eyes were like cracked ice.

"I assume you're referring to the engram matrix, sir," said Higgins, trying to keep his voice steady. "It's the term for the downloaded human personality, which is to say, not merely isolated and specific mental engram data, but the sum total of the consciousness, possibly augmented by select ancillary data. Hence, the term 'matrix.' In other words, sir, putting it in layman's terms, it's Steele's operating program.''

"That was a rather more general answer than I had in mind," said Carman in a level tone. "All that is covered in the project files you've supplied to this committee previously. I was referring to something else. Specifically, to what you refer to as *the* Matrix, with a capital 'M.' What exactly is that?"

Christ, thought Higgins. We're dead. We're fucking dead. "I suspect what you're referring to, Senator, is Steele's backup program."

"His backup program?"

"That's right, sir." You evil fucker, he thought savagely. You've got me, and you know you've got me, and now you're going to drag it out and watch me twisting in the wind.

"By backup program, I assume you're referring to what is generally known by that term, a spare copy in case something happens to the original, is that correct?"

It was pointless to struggle. Higgins locked gazes with him. "Yes, sir, that's correct, as you well know."

Carman smiled. The bastard's eyes were actually twinkling. "And where is this backup engram matrix normally kept?"

"Normally, it's kept stored in the project databanks, sir."

"Is it there now, Mr. Higgins?"

Higgins met his gaze. "No, sir. It's not."

"Where is it, then?"

Higgins compressed his lips in a tight grimace before responding. "I don't know, sir."

"You mean to say it's missing?" Carman said with feigned surprise.

Higgins stared at him with undisguised contempt. "Why don't we just cut to the chase, Senator?"

Carman smiled. "All right, Mr. Higgins. We have received sworn testimony before this committee to the effect of the following: A) In direct violation of standard practices and security procedures governing classified government research, a member of your staff, namely, Dr. Devon Cooper, working in collusion with the late Dr. Philip Gates, formerly chief engineer of your project, obtained an unauthorized copy of said backup matrix and removed it from the premises. B) The same Dr. Devon Cooper then proceeded to conduct unauthorized experiments with this illegally obtained copy of the matrix, in the process of which said matrix was brought on line and became self-aware. C) Following its being brought on line, this unauthorized copy of the matrix escaped Dr. Cooper's control and apparently, using some means which are not entirely understood, traveled through the power grid and raided the Project Download databanks, in the course of which the original backup copy of the matrix was either somehow erased or pirated. D) You now have no idea where this matrix is or who might have access to it, nor do you have any idea where Lt. Steele is. E) You have reason to believe that Steele's broadcast-link capability is malfunctioning, which prevents you from getting in touch with him, and after being informed by officers of the Metro police that it was imperative for him to contact project headquarters, Steele has not responded, which would seem to suggest the possibility of a malfunction much more serious than a breakdown of his broadcast-link capability. Do you deny any of that, Mr. Higgins?"

Holy shit, thought Higgins. He's got it all. *But how?*

"Senator, I don't know where you got your information, but—"

"That information was given to this committee in a sworn statement by a member of your project staff, Mr. Higgins."

"I'd like to know specifically who gave you that information, sir."

"Your chief cybernetics engineer, Dr. Jennifer Stone," said Carman.

Higgins felt as if he had been gut-punched. *Jennifer!* No, he thought, it was impossible. It simply couldn't be! Carman was playing some sort of game. He must have had a spy planted somewhere in the project, but even so, how could he have found out all the details. . . .

"Excuse me, Senator, but I find that rather difficult to believe."

"Would you care to see a copy of the statement?" Carman asked.

Higgins swallowed hard. "Yes, sir, I would."

Carman had it ready before him. He handed it to a page, who brought it around to Higgins. Higgins took it and quickly scanned it. The signature at the bottom was Jennifer's. There was no doubt.

"When. . . ." His voice cracked and Higgins had to clear his throat. "When was this statement given, sir?"

"About an hour and a half ago," said Carman. "Under the circumstances, the committee felt incumbent to act upon it immediately. I repeat, do you deny any of its contents?"

Higgins felt absolutely numb. Why? For God's sake, *why?* "No, sir. I do not."

"Thank you, Mr. Higgins," Carman said. "Under the circumstances, I feel that this committee has no choice but to act at once upon this information. Given the gross breaches of security, not to mention safety standards, and your failure to inform this committee of such matters, especially considering the grave threat to the public safety in light of what occurred the last time one of your cyborgs malfunctioned, I must move that Project Download be immediately suspended, pending its transfer to another, more responsible authority, and that Project Steele be immediately shut down. I must further move that both the Metropolitan Police Department and the Strike Force be immediately mobilized to locate Lt. Steele and take whatever measures are necessary to bring him in and, failing that, to take whatever steps they deem appropriate to safeguard the public safety."

"You son of a bitch!" said Higgins. "You're putting out a God damned contract on him!"

"You will control yourself, Mr. Higgins," said Carman coldly, "or I will cite you for contempt."

"You can't *do* that!" Higgins shouted, jumping to his feet. "That would be murder! You can't condemn a man without a trial!"

"Mr. Higgins! If you cannot restrain yourself, I will *have* you restrained!" said Carman. "And your colorful hyperbole notwithstanding, the fact is that Steele is not a man, he is a cyborg. His brain is a computer, and what's more, it's a computer that appears to be malfunctioning. We have a responsibility to insure the public safety, and we cannot afford a repetition of the disaster that occurred when your last cyborg ran amok. Now I will brook no further outbursts of this nature, is that clear?"

"Senator," said Higgins, struggling to compose himself, "regardless of what you may think of me, you can't do this to Steele. He's faithfully served the government of the United States, and he's saved the people of this city. He's a hero! You don't *know* that he's malfunctioning! You don't *know* that he's a threat! You can't simply condemn him without giving him a chance!''

"He'll be given every chance, Mr. Higgins. He'll be given the opportunity to come in voluntarily. However, if he refuses to comply, it will be necessary to take appropriate measures. We have the public safety to consider.''

"Public safety, my ass! It's your own goddamn agenda you're considering!''

"That's it, Higgins," Carman said. "You are in contempt. What's more, you will remain available to this committee pending a full investigation and a decision concerning the appropriate charges to be filed against yourself and Dr. Cooper and any other members of your staff who might be implicated in these violations and the subsequent coverup. Security will kindly escort Mr. Higgins from the chamber.''

"You *bastard!* You stupid, ignorant, fucking bastard—''

"Keep it up, Higgins," Carman said as security manhandled Higgins from the chamber. "Keep it up. You're just digging your own grave.''

_6_

He stood there for a moment, just looking at her. He had sprinted at least twelve city blocks at a speed an ordinary man could match only in an automobile, and he wasn't even out of breath. Still, he needed a few moments to collect himself. This was the woman he had dreamed about, the woman who had occupied his thoughts for so long, whose memory, though it wasn't really his, had filled him with such conflicting emotions. He had never met her before, yet he knew what she looked like naked. He knew how she made love. He knew the feeling of her lips on his, although they hadn't really been *his* lips, the warmth of her bare skin, the soft curves of her thighs and buttocks. He knew her mannerisms and he—or a piece of someone else named Jonathan that was now a part of him—had hurt her. Yet he was a complete stranger to her. Now that he had found her, he didn't quite know what to do.

"Excuse me, Ms. Barrett?"

She looked up at him slowly. She hadn't changed much, he thought. Her dark hair was worn longer now, falling down below her shoulders, and it didn't seem as if she paid very much attention to it. She had lost some weight, which made her high cheekbones look even more pronounced. She looked pale and drawn and her eyes were slightly glassy. She had on some tastefully applied makeup, but it didn't quite conceal the fact that she'd been doing a lot of drinking for some time. The eyes were the dead giveaway. They looked red-rimmed, hollow, empty. She was still a beautiful woman, and she was dressed well in a knee-length, tailored skirt, jacket and blouse with stockings and high heels, but she looked all used up. Steele felt powerful emotions welling up within him. His heart went out to her.

"Yes?" she said, her gaze taking time to focus on him. "Do I know you?"

"No, ma'am, not really. We've never met before. But I know who you are. I'm not trying to annoy you or pick you up or anything, but I'd really appreciate it if I could just talk to you for a few minutes. You see, in a way, a sort of unusual way, we happen to have some things in common."

"What things?" she asked.

"It's a rather long and complicated story," Steele said, "and I'm afraid it might be difficult for you. It has to do with Jonathan."

She blinked and looked away.

"Believe me, I don't want to cause you any pain, but it's important to me. Please?"

She looked back up and stared at him for a long moment.

"Lt. Steele?"

He turned to see a couple of young women standing behind him.

"Could we please have your autograph?"

Damn, thought Steele. Perfect timing. He forced a smile and said, "Sure." They handed him a couple of cocktail coasters and a pen, he asked their names and signed for them.

"Gee, thanks," one of them said. The other one made eyes at him and said, "Listen, if you're not busy, maybe you'd like to join us for a drink?"

"Thank you," Steele started to say, "I'd like to, but—"

"He's busy," Donna said.

He glanced at her with surprise.

"Well, maybe another time," one of the young women said. "It was really nice meeting you."

"Nice meeting you, too," Steele said. "Thank you."

"Please, sit down," said Donna.

He sat down in the booth across from her. Almost immediately, Rick came over personally and asked him if he'd like a drink or something to eat.

"Just coffee, please," said Steele.

"Sure thing, Steele. Comin' right up."

"I thought you looked vaguely familiar," Donna said. "I've seen you on the news. You worked with Jonathan?"

"Was he a cop?"

She frowned. "I thought you said you knew him."

"In a sense, I do," said Steele. "In some ways, I'm very close to him. But we've never met and up until a short while ago, I couldn't even remember his last name."

She looked confused. "I don't understand."

"You said you've seen me on the news," said Steele. "How much do you know about me?"

She shrugged. "I know that you're the famous cyborg

who helped avert a military coup. I've seen you on TV and I've seen your picture in the papers and on the covers of some magazines. Other than that, I don't really know very much about you at all.''

"I, on the other hand, know a great deal about you," Steele said. "I know how you broke up with Jonathan Barrett and why. I know you've had a real hard time. I know you have a small birthmark underneath your left breast—"

"How on earth do you know that? Jonathan told you?"

"I remember," Steele said.

Rick brought him the coffee and left.

Donna frowned again. "I thought you said we never met. And if you've ever seen me with my shirt off, I should think that I'd remember *that*."

"In order to explain, I need to tell you a little bit about myself," said Steele. "I used to be a Strike Force cop. I managed to annoy my chief once too often and he 'volunteered' me as a subject for a classified government experiment, something called Project Download. It was an experiment to test brain/computer interface. They implanted a tiny biochip in my brain so that they could have me do certain things and record the process on computer, to see if they could download various types of knowledge and abilities. They can, incidentally. Anyway, the biochip was a permanent implant. Shortly after I participated in the experiments, I went back to active duty and ran into an ambush. I was shot up pretty bad and left for dead inside a burning building. By the time they pulled me out, there wasn't much left of me. I was still alive, just barely, but my injuries were extensive and severe and I was in a coma, with brain damage. Essentially, a vegetable. But the biochip was still functioning. So they used it to download my personality, my identity, and store it in a computer. While they repaired my body and made me into a cyborg, they also started working on repairing my personality. Some engram data had been lost due to brain damage, and to compensate for that, they filled in with some ancillary engram data that they'd recorded from some other test subjects who'd participated in the Download experiments. Then they installed an artificial brain in my head and programmed it with my human personality. Is this confusing for you?''

She shook her head, looking interested. ''No, go on.''

''Well, I woke up feeling the same way I always did, except I was a cyborg. Part man and part machine. With an artificial brain. I still had the same identity, the same personality, the same memories, only the essence of what I had been was now contained in a cybernetic brain instead of an organic one. That . . . took a bit of getting used to.''

''God, I should think so,'' she said.

''In some ways, I'm still not really used to it,'' said Steele, ''but that's not all. Not long after I 'came on line,' as they call it, I started having dreams. Strange, frightening, inexplicable dreams. Recurring nightmares. One of them, the one I had most often, was about you.''

''About *me?*''

''I've had several different dreams about you, but this one particular dream kept coming back to me, night after night. I was in a park, having a picnic with my wife and children. Now, I'd been married—I'm divorced now—and my wife's name was Janice. She was a blonde. And I had two children. A boy and a girl, Jason and Cory. Teenagers. My daughter was . . . she died recently.''

''I heard about that. I'm sorry.''

''Anyway,'' Steele continued, ''they weren't the people in my dream. In my dream, the children weren't Jason and

Cory. I didn't know who they were. They were smaller, younger. Twin boys and a girl. And in the dream, my wife wasn't a blonde. She was a brunette. And her name wasn't Janice. It was Donna.''

Donna Barrett was staring at him with a stunned expression.

"I was playing with the children, when suddenly, a screamer appeared and attacked them. There was nothing I could do to stop it. I don't know why, but in the dream, I couldn't seem to move. You were screaming hysterically—''

"*Stop*,'' hissed Donna. She closed her eyes. Her lower lip was trembling. "For God's sake, please stop.''

Steele stopped. He hated putting her through this, but there was just no other way.

After a moment, she opened her eyes and looked at him with a dazed expression.

"How could you possibly know about that?'' she asked.

"At first, I *didn't* know,'' said Steele. "I couldn't account for it. I couldn't understand it. I had other dreams about you. One of them took place right here, in this bar, in this very booth. We were here together. And you were crying because I'd just told you that I was leaving you.''

She was shaking her head slowly, barely perceptibly, and staring at him with a stricken expression. "My God. You were dreaming my *life!*''

"No,'' said Steele gently. "Not *your* life. Jonathan's. I couldn't understand it. It was driving me crazy. I thought maybe I was losing my mind.'' He paused. "Maybe I am. Because, you see, what happened was when they used that ancillary data to fill out my engram matrix, my identity, to compensate for the brain damage, they used engram data from other test subjects that they'd worked with. It was only supposed to compensate for function loss, but it did much more. It became a part of my subconscious. A part of *me*. I was remembering bits and pieces of other people's lives. I was having memories of experiences I'd never actually had, but in a way, I *did* have them, because they had become a part of me. Part of my identity. Jonathan Barrett wasn't the only one, but his personality fragment is the strongest. He must have been one of the test subjects in the Download experiments. They used recordings of some of his mental engrams to repair me. Parts of Jonathan are now a part of me. He's like a ghost inside my mind. And until this moment, so were you.''

She said nothing. She just continued staring at him as if . . . . as if she'd seen a ghost, thought Steele.

"I don't know if I can explain this to you," Steele said, "but I have to try. You see, I knew you weren't my wife. I knew I'd never met you, but I *knew* you. I felt . . . *connected* to you. I couldn't help it. This may sound crazy, but I felt as if you really were my wife, as if your children were *our* children. And after the tragic thing that happened. . . ." He paused. "I'm sorry. I know this can't be easy for you. But you see, I lost my entire family in exactly the same way."

Her eyes were damp. "You did?" she said softly.

"My mother was a nurse," said Steele. "I was just a kid then. She was working with some doctors who were trying to find a cure for Virus 3 and she got infected by a sample of contaminated blood. It must have happened very quickly. She was already a screamer when she got home. I had two younger brothers. . . . about the same age as your twins were when it happened . . . and she attacked them. She didn't know what she was doing, of course; she was hopelessly insane. By the time my father got to them, she'd already infected them. She attacked him and they struggled and my dad broke a chair over her back and stunned her; then he got out his .45 and shot her.''

"My God.''

Steele nodded. ''I was petrified. I couldn't move. Until that shot. When he fired the gun, I screamed. I wanted to run to him, but he yelled at me to stay away. He'd never yelled at me like that before. He wasn't angry. He was scared. See, he'd become infected, too. And he knew he didn't have much time. He told me that I'd have to be brave and be a man and that he hoped someday I'd understand what he was about to do. He said after he did it, I had to call the police and explain to them what happened and under no circumstances to touch them or come near them. . . . and then he called my brothers over. . . . they were crying . . . and he hugged them and kissed them and told them to turn around and then he shot them both. Quickly. One bullet each through the back of the head. Then he stuck the gun into his mouth and blew his brains out.''

"Oh, Jesus,'' Donna said. "And you *saw* it all?''

Steele nodded. He hadn't touched his coffee. She hadn't touched her drink.

"How old were you?'' she asked.

"Sixteen,'' said Steele. ''Anyway, in the dream, it was my mother who attacked our children . . . *your* children . . . and it wasn't Jonathan who was there, but *me*. And I just stood there, helpless, unable to do anything, just the way I had when my mom attacked my brothers.''

"That's what Jonathan did,'' said Donna softly. ''He didn't do anything.'' She looked away. ''Only he didn't just stand there. He ran away. The screamer who attacked our children was a woman. An old woman. I know they're very strong when they're like that, but she was an *old woman*. And Jonathan just ran away. I was the one who drove her off.''

"*You?*" said Steele.

She still wasn't looking at him. "I just went crazy. I picked up the picnic basket and started hitting her with it, swinging it with all my might, just screaming at her and hitting her and hitting her until she took off. . . .''

"You could have been killed," said Steele.

"I didn't care. She was hurting my *children*." Donna swallowed hard. She seemed to be staring at something beyond the bare brick wall, as if she could see through it. "After she ran off, Jonathan came back and said we had to take the kids to the hospital right away. He didn't say anything else at all until we got there. He didn't even look at me. And when we got there, these men . . . they were dressed all in padding, like those people who work with attack dogs . . . they took the children, and I realized what they were going to do. I know they had no choice. And I know that it was better for them to die that way than to . . . to be like. . . .''

She looked back at Steele and he saw tears streaming down her cheeks.

" He ran away," she said in a hollow voice. "He just . . . ran away.''

"So that's why he left you," Steele said quietly. "He couldn't take the guilt.''

"Say, excuse me, I hate to interrupt, but aren't you Donovan Steele, the cyborg?''

Steele looked up to see a man standing by the table. He had no idea how long he'd been there. "Please," he said, "not now.''

"Yeah, I told my buddies it was you! Listen, it would

be great if we could tell the guys back in the office that we arm-wrestled with you. How about it?''

''Look, fella, give me a break, will you? I'm having a private conversation here.''

''Hey, come on, it'll only take a minute. Whaddya say?''

''Let's get out of here,'' said Donna, reaching for her purse.

''Oh, come on, man, don't leave. It'll only take a minute.''

''I'm sorry,'' Steele said, getting up.

''Check please,'' Donna said to a passing waitress.

''Oh, no,'' the waitress said. ''It's all taken care of. Any friend of Steele's . . . ''

Steele took out his wallet and dropped a ten onto the table.

''Hey, how about it, Steele? Whaddya say?''

''Take me out of here,'' said Donna.

''Oh, come on, sister, you got all night with him. Nothing that won't wait a minute, right?'' He winked at Steele.

Steele grabbed him by the shirtfront, and his eyes glowed red as his laser designator switched in.

''The lady wants to leave,'' he said, ''and you're being a real pain in the ass.''

The man paled. ''Hey, okay, no problem! Take it easy!''

He released the man and headed for the door with Donna.

''Jesus Christ!'' the man said, swallowing hard. His eyes followed Steele as he went out the door, then he glanced around at everybody in the bar. They were all looking at him. ''Did you *see* that? Man! You try to be friendly and the guy almost takes your head off! What an asshole!''

''You're the asshole, friend,'' said Rick from behind the bar. ''Man's got a right to privacy and you were bothering

him and the lady. Now do me a favor and leave, okay?
Forget the check. Just don't come back.''

She wasn't at the lab or in her office. She'd left for the
day. There was no answer at her apartment, either, and on
the ninth or tenth ring, Higgins realized where she would
be. She wasn't the type to run and hide. They were alike
in that respect. Both aggressive, both implacable, both relentless. Both people who took the bull by the horns and
wrestled it to the ground, come hell or high water. She was
waiting for him in the living room of his apartment. She'd
let herself in with her key. Higgins noticed that she'd had
a few drinks. A half-empty glass and a bottle of Scotch
stood on the coffee table by the couch. She stood up as he
came in, a determined expression on her face. Higgins' own
face was white with stone-cold fury.

''*What have you done?*''

''What I had to do,'' she answered calmly. A half a bottle
of whiskey, but her voice was steady and her eyes were
clear.

''*Why?*''

''We couldn't go on like this,'' she said in a level tone.
''We'd lost control. Steele is acting erratically. What happened to Stalker is probably already happening to him.''

''God damn it, you don't *know* that!''

''If I had waited until I knew it for sure, it would probably
be too late,'' she replied. ''I'm chief engineer on this project, and I have my responsibilities. He's refused to come
in and have his programming debugged, and now he's refusing to come in at all. He's simply disappeared, and no
one has any idea where he is. It's probably already started.
Then there's the Matrix. It's doing the same thing. It's
disintegrating, just like Steele is. It's not sane, Oliver.

It's threatened you. It's threatened *us*. And your answer to that was to knuckle in to its demands, the demands of a *computer program*, for God's sake, and then *order* me into therapy with Dev Cooper. As if *I* was the one who was the problem!''

"Jesus Christ, Jennifer, I did that for your sake! And I was going to see Cooper, too. We've both been under a lot of strain and I needed to be sure we were making the right decisions. I'd already *started* seeing him!''

"Wonderful,'' she said flatly. "Did he give you a critique of our sex life?''

Higgins stared at her with astonishment. "I can't believe it,'' he said, stunned. "That's what it's really all about, isn't it? The Matrix taped us while we were screwing and Dev Cooper caught a brief glimpse of it and now they've got to pay, is that it?''

"Don't be crude,'' she said with distaste.

"Crude? *Crude?* My God, do you even realize what you've *done?* You've ruined his life! He's probably going to go to *prison!* And maybe *I* will, too!''

"You're not going to go to prison,'' she said, as if patiently explaining to a child. "That was part of the deal I made with Carman.''

"Deal? *What* deal?''

"In exchange for my cooperating with the committee and giving them that statement, he's promised to give you nothing more than an official reprimand and keep Download intact after he shuts down Project Steele. It will be transferred to Los Alamos, and I'll be made director of the project. It will be just like we talked about when you thought they were going to shut down the project and disband the agency. We'll leave this lousy city and move to New Mexico, where you can breathe fresh air and see trees instead of filthy, crumbling buildings, and we can have a decent life together. A *good* life.''

''Well, that's just great,'' said Higgins with disbelief. ''And what about Dev Cooper?''

''I don't know why you're being so concerned about him,'' she said flatly. ''It was Dev Cooper who brought all this down on us. If it hadn't been for him, we wouldn't have this problem with the Matrix. And he not only refused to cooperate in having Steele's programming debugged, he violated regulations by stealing highly classified data. I'm at a loss to understand why you're being so protective of him. If it had been anybody else, you would have had them arrested.''

Higgins shook his head in amazement. ''You've got it all figured out, haven't you?'' he said. ''You've got it all neatly rationalized away. The Matrix is an insane computer program that has to be destroyed, and Cooper is a criminal who has to be punished, just because they caught you with your pants off.''

''You're being ridiculous.''

''And what about Steele? What's *he* done to you? He's out there, afraid to come in because he thinks he might be losing it. He doesn't know about the Matrix, so he has no way of knowing that he *wasn't* hearing things, that it really *was* his own voice on that phone! There's probably nothing wrong with him at all, only he doesn't know that! Except now, thanks to you, they're going to hunt him down and try to kill him. And for *what?* Because he wouldn't let you play around with his software? Because you resent him for being able to have an open relationship with a former hooker while you, the distinguished and respected scientist, have to sneak around to play your kinky sex games behind closed doors? God forbid anyone should find out that you like to get your legs up in the air like any other woman!''

"I'm not going to react to that. You're just angry because I took control of the situation and went over your head," said Jennifer. "If you think about it clearly for a moment, you'll realize that I was right and that I did what I did because it was necessary, not because I was trying to threaten your masculinity. And I also did it for *you*, Oliver. It was all coming apart, and if I hadn't gone to Carman when I did, your head would have been on the chopping block, along with mine. I've worked all my life to get to where I am today. I wasn't about to watch both my career and yours go down the drain simply because some misguided loyalties and your male ego wouldn't allow you to admit that some serious mistakes had been made. I did it for *us*, Oliver."

"There is no 'us' anymore," said Higgins, staring at her as if he were seeing her for the first time, *really* seeing her. "You killed it, Jennifer, along with everything else I've worked so hard to achieve. But you don't understand that, do you? You really don't. You've got it all worked out so that everything dovetails neatly in your twisted logic."

"You're being melodramatic," she said.

"Melodramatic? You've just destroyed two men, Jennifer. And you've destroyed me, too. I trusted you. I *loved* you. And in one fell swoop, you took the project away from me, gave Carman what he needs to have the agency disbanded, sent Dev Cooper to prison and condemned Steele to death. Melodramatic? Jesus, melodramatic doesn't even come close. You're a ruthless, terrifying, cold-hearted fucking bitch, and it makes my blood run cold to think I've been inside you."

She stiffened. "You're only striking out at me because your pride's been hurt. You're incapable of being objective about this right now. I did the only thing I could do to try to salvage everything we've worked for, but if trying to hurt my feelings is going to help you get this out of your system, then—''

"Hurt your *feelings?*" Higgins said with disbelief. "My God. Get out, Jennifer. Get out before I lose what little self-control I've got left."

"All right," she said. "If that's what you really want, I'll leave. We'll talk about this after you've had a chance to calm down and think this over. But I want you to know that you're not being very fair to me. If you were really honest with yourself, you'd see that taking your frustration out on me is—''

Higgins lunged at her and grabbed her by the throat with both hands. He spun her around and forced her backward as she clawed at his hands and made choking sounds. He slammed her back against the door, hard, then pulled her back, flung open the door and shoved her out into the hallway hard enough to send her sprawling. She fell to the floor and stayed there, clutching at her throat and coughing, gasping hoarsely for breath.

"Get out of my sight," said Higgins, "because so help me God, if I ever lay eyes on you again, I'll fucking kill you."

He slammed the door shut and leaned back against it, shutting his eyes and breathing deeply, trying to get himself back under control, fighting a powerful urge to go after her and make good his threat. After a moment, his breathing slowed, and he went over to the coffee table, picked up the bottle of Scotch and took a long pull on it. Then he drew his arm back and threw the bottle against the wall with all his might. He put his hand up to his forehead and held it there, fingers pressing in against his temples as if to counteract the pressure from inside that threatened to build up and explode. Then he took another deep breath and exhaled it slowly.

"No, goddamnit!" he said through gritted teeth. "I ain't fucking rollin' over on this. Not by a long shot."

He snatched up the phone and punched out Dev Cooper's number.

It was a tiny apartment, a railroad flat laid out in a succession of three rooms, with the entrance leading into a small kitchen with ancient and battered appliances and a small wood table with two chairs. A short hallway that was little more than a walk-through closet led into another small room that she had turned into a sort of den with bookshelves and a writing desk, with a bathroom in the corner no larger than a closet, just barely enough room to accommodate the toilet, sink and bathtub with a showerhead. Off the den there was a living room with a well-worn and faded throw rug on the floor, a few more bookshelves, a fireplace, a couple of chairs, a couch of the type that unfolded into a bed, a reading lamp and an old stained and scratched-up coffee table. The bookshelves were nothing more than boards placed across stacks of bricks. They were crammed with a profusion of old hardcovers and aging paperbacks. The living room had the apartment's only windows, but they had been boarded up. The boards looked fairly heavy, and there were crossbraces hammered into them on the inside. The place wasn't much different from the ramshackle apartments found in no-man's-land, except she had power and running water. And though it was hardly what anyone could call luxurious or even very comfortable, it was neat and tidy. Nothing was out of place.

"It's not much, but it's home," said Donna with a self-deprecating shrug. "Would you like a drink?"

"If it's no trouble."

"No trouble at all. I haven't got much in the way of food, but booze I've got. Scotch all right?"

"Scotch would be fine."

"I don't have any soda."

"I take it neat."

She got out a bottle and two glasses. "You know, it just occurred to me, what happens when you drink?"

"Nothing much," said Steele. "I can't get drunk. I don't have to worry about damaging any brain cells, though if I drank enough, I suppose I could screw up my liver."

"So what's the point? If you can't even get a buzz, I mean?"

"I don't drink to get drunk."

"No? I do."

She sat down on the couch beside him and filled their glasses.

"Cheers."

They drank.

"I'm sorry about what happened back there," Steele said.

"I suppose it comes with being famous," she said.

"I didn't mean that," he said. "I meant about making you cry."

"I haven't been able to cry in a long time," she said. "It helps, you know."

"I know. I can't do it."

"A lot of men can't."

"No, I mean I'm physically incapable of crying. My eyes are bionic optic units."

She stared at them. She hadn't seen it when his laser designator switched in back at the bar. "They look perfectly normal."

"Most of me does," he said. "A lot of me is. But then, a lot of me isn't, either."

"What parts are . . . I'm sorry. I don't mean to be rude."

"It's all right. What parts are artificial, you mean? My brain, of course. My skull is made of nysteel. Both my arms and legs. My ears. My eyes. My jaw and teeth. My skeletal system is either nysteel or reinforced with nysteel. The skin over most of my body is a polymer compound that's bullet resistant . . ."

She touched his hand.

"It feels like ordinary skin," she said.

"Yeah," he said, "they're pretty good at that."

"Can you feel that?" she said, running her finger along the back of his hand.

"Yep. Microsensors. I'm state-of-the-art."

She turned his hand over. "What's that?" she asked, pointing to the circular indentation in his palm.

"Gun port. Retractable 10 mm. semiautomatic pistol. I've got a carbon laser in the other one," he said, holding up his other hand. "You're sitting here with a walking arsenal. Make you feel nervous?"

She shook her head. "How does it make *you* feel?"

"Strange," he said. "Sometimes, I don't feel human. I'm not sure if I am."

"You seem very human to me," she said softly. "If you weren't, I don't think you could feel about things the way you do."

"I'm not even sure about that," said Steele. "You heard about what happened to the second cyborg that they built? The one called Stalker?"

She nodded.

"He used to be my partner," Steele said. "His name was Mick Taylor. He's the one who introduced me to my

ex-wife.'' He paused. Was it dangerous for him to be alone
with her? He seemed to be all right now, but how could he
be sure? "He went insane. I'm not sure the same thing's
not happening to me.''

"Because of the dreams, you mean? Your memories
about me?''

"Jonathan's memories.''

"No," she said, "*your* memories. Maybe you got them
from Jonathan, but they're yours now. Ours," she added
softly. "You're nothing like him."

"Would it bother you to tell me about him?''

"No. Not anymore.''

"What is he like?''

"Was," she said.

"I'm sorry?''

"He's dead.''

"I didn't know.''

"He killed himself. About a year ago. God, has it been
a year? He worked for the government. He was a program-
mer.''

"You mean he worked on the project?'' Steele said,
stunned that Jonathan could have been so close.

"I'm not sure what he really did," she said. She
shrugged. "Something at the Federal Building. He said it
was classified, he couldn't talk about it. He kept a lot of
things bottled up inside. He was a good man, but he wasn't
very strong. It was probably my fault he died.''

"How was it your fault?''

"I blamed him for what happened to the children," she
said dully. "For running away and not doing anything to
stop it. After it happened, I had a breakdown. They kept
me in the hospital for a while. He tried to come and see
me, but I said I didn't want to see him and they wouldn't

let him in. I found out later he was sleeping with my sister. Maybe he did it because he was lonely and depressed. Maybe he did it to get back at me. I don't know, maybe it had been going on much longer than I thought. With Trudy, anything was possible.''

Steele suddenly had an image of a girl about five years younger than Donna and bearing a strong resemblance to her, but with a more stubborn, willful expression, a sultry, pouting mouth and a rebellious, challenging look about the eyes.

''Shortly after I came home from the hospital,'' she said, ''he moved out. I guess I knew then that he was going to leave me. I drove him away. I was a constant reminder to him of what had happened, of how he had panicked and run away, abandoning his children. . . . I guess he couldn't live with that.''

''That doesn't make it your fault,'' said Steele.

''It's my fault that I couldn't forgive him and try to help him through it. I loved him. But I just couldn't forgive him.''

''Can you forgive yourself?'' asked Steele.

She looked up at him and blinked.

''You didn't *do* anything, Donna,'' Steele said. ''You were a victim of a terrible tragedy. Things like that happen, but they're not anybody's fault. Hell, it wasn't even the screamer's fault. The screamer was a victim, too. Life can be really hard sometimes. Brutally hard. But that doesn't mean you have to find someone to blame for it. Or blame yourself because you could have done things differently. That's got nothing to do with reality. Reality is what happened. It's what *is*, not what might have been. I guess Jonathan didn't really understand that. He didn't solve anything by killing himself. He just passed the buck. Like a little boy saying, 'Look what you made me do.' Crawling into a bottle won't solve anything, either. It won't make the pain go away. It might keep you from feeling it for a while, but it'll still be there when you get sober, and then you'll just have to get drunk again to hide from it, only you can't hide from yourself. The way to deal with pain, Donna, is to allow yourself to *feel* it. Pain is one of the things that makes us human, that lets us know we're still alive. It's all right to hurt.''

"It's hard," she said. A single tear started a track down her cheek.

"I know," he said. "But it's harder if you hide from it. Believe me, I know. I've been there."

She reached out and gently touched his cheek, then suddenly she was sobbing. Great, wailing, wracking sobs that shook her entire body. Steele put his arms around her, and she buried her head in his shoulder as all her repressed grief finally broke through.

"It's okay," he said, stroking her hair gently. "Just let it out. Let it all out."

She cried for what seemed like a long time, then finally she started to quiet down. The flood gates had burst, and the grief and pain had all flowed out, and now there was only a trickle left. For a while, they simply held each other as she cried softly, then she pulled away and looked at him. She brought her face to his and kissed him. He could taste the salt of her tears.

"Donna. . . ." he said. "I'm *not* Jonathan."

"I know," she said. "It's not Jonathan I want." And she kissed him again. They sank back down onto the couch.

7

Raven opened the door of the apartment to admit Dev Cooper. "Dev! What is it? Have you heard from Steele?"

"Pack," he said, brushing past her.

"What?"

"I said, *pack*," he repeated urgently. "Pack your things. We haven't got much time."

"Pack my things? I don't understand. What *is* this? What's going on?"

"*Listen* to me," he said, grabbing her by the shoulders. "Higgins just called me a little while ago. Carman's found out about the Matrix and about Steele taking off on us. It's hit the fan."

"Senator Carman?" she said, looking confused. "But how could he—"

"Jennifer Stone went to him and told him the whole story. She sold us out. Carman just had Higgins up before the damn committee. They're shutting down Project Steele and taking over Download. There's probably an order going out for my arrest right now. What's more, Carman's putting out an APB on Steele."

"*What?* That's crazy! Why?"

"The official story is that Steele's malfunctioning, and both the Metro police and Strike Force are being mobilized to bring him in. If he won't come in voluntarily, they've got orders to take whatever steps are necessary to neutralize him. You understand what that means?"

"Holy shit. I don't believe it!"

"*Believe* it. Higgins is on his way over here right now. Where does Steele keep his gear, his weapons and his battle mods?"

"In the arms cabinet, over there . . . "

"I'll take care of it," said Cooper. "Pack your stuff."

"I don't have any suitcases—"

"Take what you can and wrap it in a fuckin' blanket, girl! Use pillow cases, anything, but get your shit together! *Move* it!"

Without another word, she ran into the bedroom. Dev went over to the arms cabinet and opened it. He started taking out Steele's battle mods, the modular appendages and the special belt they attached to, the guns and the spare magazines and the holsters, dumping it all out onto the floor and taking a quick inventory. If he forgot anything, there'd be no chance to come back for it. Outside, he heard the sounds of a chopper coming into the penthouse helipad. Moments later, Higgins and two of his agents came in through the sliding glass doors.

"That all the stuff?" asked Higgins.

"I think that's all of it," Cooper replied.

Higgins checked it all over quickly. "Okay, it's all here. Sharp, Foster, pack it up."

Agents Sharp and Foster started packing the gear away as quickly as they could in a couple of large duffle bags.

"Where's Raven?" Higgins asked.

"In the bedroom, getting her things together," Cooper said.

"Hell, it'll take her all day," said Higgins. "Sharp, go help her."

Sharp grabbed one of the spare duffles and went into the bedroom.

"How much time have we got?" asked Cooper.

"I don't know," Higgins replied. "But Carman will probably move fast. I've got King and Matson over at your place, packing your things. They're just going to take some clothes and a few personal effects, plus your notes and records. Whatever they think's important."

"My notes and records are the only things that matter," Dev said. "Where are we going?"

"You'll find out when we get there. *Sharp!* Let's move it!"

The bedroom door opened and Sharp came out with Raven. He was carrying a duffel filled with her clothing. Foster had already gone out to load Steele's gear in the chopper.

"All right, you know what to do?" asked Higgins.

"Stay here and wait for word from Ice," said Sharp. "If he calls, let him know what's happened. Otherwise, alert security downstairs and stay in touch with the units outside so they can pick him up before he comes anywhere near the building. If anyone else shows up and tries to get in, stall."

"Right," said Higgins. "Another chopper should be coming in in about five minutes. I'll have it standing by on the pad outside. If you can't stall them any longer, get out of here. I don't want them arresting you for obstruction."

"Got it."

"Okay, let's move."

"Wait! Where are we *going?*" Raven asked.

"I've got no time for explanations," Higgins said. "If you want to help Steele, shut up and do what you're told. Now come on, let's move it!"

"You've gotta be kidding me," said Jake Hardesty with disbelief.

"It's no joke, Jake," the commissioner said over the phone. "This comes right from the top. You're to mobilize all units to find Steele and bring him in. And if he won't come voluntarily, your orders are to take whatever steps are necessary."

"What the hell does *that* mean?"

"I don't think I have to spell it out for you, do I, Jake?"

"Commissioner, I'm going to *insist* you spell it out," said Hardesty with an edge to his voice.

There was a brief, uneasy silence. "All right, Jake. I owe you that much, at least. He was one of your people. If Steele resists arrest, use of deadly force is authorized."

"Jesus Christ," said Hardesty. "Sir, I'd like to know who gave that order."

"*I'm* giving the order, Jake."

"You know what I mean," Hardesty replied. "Who's leaning on you?"

"You're out of line, Jake."

"Don't give me that! Damn it, I've got a right to know! Is Higgins behind this?"

"I told you, Jake, this order comes down from the top. I got it from the mayor and he got it direct from Congress."

"Congress! You mean Bryce Carman, don't you?"

"You can draw whatever inference you like," the commissioner said. "The point is, you've got your orders."

"If I give an order like that to my people, I'm liable to have a mutiny on my hands," said Hardesty.

"In that case, I suggest you remind them of what happened with the other cyborg," the commissioner said.

"What proof do we have that Steele's malfunctioning?" asked Hardesty. "None of the units have reported anything. There's been no word from the street."

"We can't afford to wait for that," the commissioner replied. "And the decision isn't mine to make, Jake. I've got my orders, too. Steele has disappeared. Word is, he's acting erratically and when he encountered a Metro unit that gave him orders to come in, he refused. If he goes off the deep end the same way Stalker did, we're going to have a real mess on our hands. If that's the case, then remember that it isn't Steele anymore, but a machine that's out of control. A very dangerous machine. He's got to be brought in. And if he won't come in, he's got to be stopped."

"God *damn* it," Hardesty said. "What does Higgins have to say about this?"

"Not that it's any of your business, but it's out of his hands," said the commissioner. "Project Steele has been ordered shut down and Download's been taken away from the agency due to flagrant security violations and an attempt to cover them up. I wouldn't want to be in Oliver Higgins' shoes right now. Or Dr. Cooper's, for that matter. I've just issued orders to Metro to have him brought in on charges of criminal conspiracy. The whole thing's a mess, and Steele is right smack in the middle of it. Find him, Jake. Find him and convince him to come in quietly. For everybody's sake.''

The commissioner hung up the phone.

"*Jesus fucking Christ!*" said Hardesty. He slammed down the receiver.

Steele stared at the naked woman asleep beside him in the bed. He thought of Raven. It was the first time he had ever been unfaithful to her. Not that they had ever promised to be faithful to each other. They had never bothered to strictly define their relationship. They had simply taken things one day at a time, and it had seemed to work that way. Raven had felt threatened by Donna the ghost. He wondered how she'd feel about Donna as a reality.

Strangely, he didn't feel guilty. He felt as if perhaps he should, but he didn't. What had just happened had seemed right, somehow. It had felt right, two people reaching out to one another, trying to establish contact, to find reassurance and some kind of meaning, each trying to lay their ghosts to rest. He looked down at Donna's body, so different from Raven's. Fuller. Softer. More mature. She had made love differently, too. With Raven, it was always very passionate and energetic. Even better than it had been with Janice, and he had not thought that it *could* be better than it had been with Janice. But with Donna, it had been different.

They had started off slowly, with great tenderness and a certain hesitancy, as if neither of them were really sure what they were doing. Donna had never taken her eyes from his. There had been a desperate intensity in her gaze, a longing, a searching, and behind it, clearly mirrored, there was so much pain. . . .

It startled him how familiar and natural it felt. He knew

her and he knew her body as if he had made love to her a thousand times. When they kissed, her full, pliant lips gently tasting his, it felt unbelievably familiar. Yet he'd never even touched her before. It was an incredible sensation. He knew the precise spot on her neck where she liked being kissed, knew exactly how it affected her when he took her erect nipples between his lips and gently sucked on them, touching them ever so lightly with his teeth. He knew how to run his fingertips gently down the curve of her spine, tracing the vertibrae down to the small of her back and pressing her buttocks up against him. It was like a well choreographed dance with an old lover as they lay locked together, on their sides, facing one another, her eyes wide and staring at him, marveling at his knowledge of her, stunned at a complete stranger making love to her exactly as her husband had once done. He had caught himself doing it and thought to do it differently, afraid of the effect that it would have on her, but she had realized what he was thinking and had stopped him by placing her fingers up against his cheek and shaking her head, saying softly, "No, don't stop." And he knew precisely what she meant.

He had realized that just as he was trying to connect with her and to resolve his doubts and his uncertainties, to experience a vital part of his past for the first time, so she was trying to do the same. In a way, she was finally saying goodbye to Jonathan. To his memory, which had haunted her as her memory had haunted Steele. He never had the feeling that she was trying to pretend she was making love with Jonathan. He was intensely aware of her being with *him*, with a stranger named Donovan Steele, who was, in a surreal way, both a stranger and an old lover. She kept looking up at him and touching him, exploring his body with her fingertips as if to reassure herself of his reality, and at the same time, he had the sense that she knew Jonathan was there as well, or at least a part of him was—as if she were making love to two men in the same body.

He had moved on top of her and raised her legs up, gently kissing her ankles and the insides of her calves, then he had placed her legs over his shoulders and entered her, penetrating deeply as she gasped and closed her eyes and softly said, "Oh, God. . . ." She kept saying, "Yes, oh, yes," as he moved inside her until she shuddered violently and exploded in multiple orgasms, making a low, keening noise way back in her throat. Then she brought her hands up and cupped his face, pulling it down to her and kissing him deeply, with astonishing fervor, with the desperation of someone who had been alone and hurting for a long, long time.

Afterward, they lay on their sides, facing one another, simply staring into one another's eyes as she gently stroked his cheek and he caressed her. It seemed that words needed to be said, but no words would fit and they both knew that. The moment was too fragile. Speaking would only break the spell.

After a while, she closed her eyes and fell asleep, nestled up against him. Steele remained awake, puzzled at the way he felt. He felt neither guilt nor regret, but a profound contentment and a great sense of relief. She was *real* to him now. Together, they had both completed something, something that had been incomplete and unresolved in each of them, in different ways, for a long time.

Steele did not know how he knew, but somehow, he was certain that the nightmare in the park would never trouble him again. Jonathan's past and Donna's past and his own past had all merged. There were no more unanswered questions. The specters had been laid to rest. Would Raven understand? He thought she would.

"Who is she?" Donna said.

He glanced at her, startled. She was lying there, awake and watching him.

"What?"

"The girl you're thinking of. Who is she?"

"Her name is Raven."

"It's a pretty name."

"She's a pretty girl. In a hardened sort of way," he added.

"Hardened? Why do you say that?"

"She hasn't had a very easy life."

"Tell me about her."

"You ever hear of the Borodini Enclave?"

"The settlement controlled by the crime family in Long Island?"

"That's the one. Out in Cold Spring Harbor. She was born there. I don't really know much about her family. What happened to them, I mean. She was orphaned at an early age and she never talks about it. There are a lot of things she never talks about."

Donna nodded with understanding. She knew about hurt held inside.

"When she was about fourteen or so, she caught the eye of Tommy Borodini."

"Victor Borodini's son? The one they used to call Tommy B?"

"That's him. He must have been about twenty-eight at the time. Tommy always liked them young. Anyway, he took her in. They became lovers and she became part of the family. The inner circle. Apparently, there was talk of marriage, but I don't know how serious it was. For Tommy,

I mean. It was serious for Raven. She loved him. And then one day she caught him with another girl. One of her friends. She walked in on them and Tommy made a joke of it. Wanted her to join them and make it a threesome. There was an argument and he struck her. She cut him with a knife. Slashed his face. You didn't do that to Tommy the Bug. He beat her half to death, then turned her over to some of his goons. Sat there and watched while they raped her."

"My God."

"It gets worse. After they were through with her, he had them drive her to the city, out to no-man's-land, up north in Harlem, and turn her over to a sadistic pimp named Rico. Part of their prostitution operation. Rico turned her out. Made her part of his stable of hookers."

"Jesus. Couldn't she run away?"

"It's not that easy," Steele said. "For one thing, she had nowhere to go. She didn't know anybody in the city. For another, she had been brutalized, and Rico kept her at his place for a while, until she looked presentable enough to turn tricks. And he worked on her during all that time. I've seen it more often than I care to think about. The players, as they call themselves, like to boast that there's no defense against a master pimp. They may be right. In their own primitive way, they're experts at brainwashing. They take impressionable young girls, girls who are vulnerable, and systematically destroy their personalities. Strip them of their dignity. Make them feel worthless and dependent. You'd be surprised at how easily it can be done."

"No," said Donna quietly, "I don't think I'd be surprised."

"Rico kept her for some years," continued Steele, "but she always gave him trouble. A part of her had never completely submitted to him. She never forgot what Tommy did to her. She held onto that, nurturing the memory, cherishing it in a perverse sort of way, letting it grow cold and hard inside her. Someday, somehow, she was determined to get even with him. And she kept rebelling against Rico. He kept sending her out to trick for some pretty twisted johns and she got hurt. She hurt a few of them back. Cut them with a knife. Rico finally decided to cut her loose, but he couldn't get any other pimp to take her. They all knew she was trouble. So, since he couldn't turn a profit on her, he gave her to the Skulls. To use and discard when they'd had their fun. The night we met, me and my partner, Ice, were conducting a raid on one of Borodini's warehouses. The Skulls were working for him. They had Raven in the warehouse and they were gang raping her. We pulled her out of there, took care of the Skulls and Borodini's men, then blew up the warehouse. She'd been worked over pretty well, and I wanted to take her to the hospital, but she refused. I suppose I could have taken her there anyway, but I figured she'd been through enough, so I took her home with me.''

He smiled. ''The first night, she tried to kill me.''

''To *kill* you?'' Donna asked with astonishment. ''After you saved her from that gang?''

''Sounds strange, doesn't it?'' said Steele. ''But it made sense in a way. I sort of expected it. After I brought her home and she got cleaned up, she tried to show her appreciation in the only way she knew how. When I didn't take her up on it, she figured me for a sucker. And in her world, suckers deserved everything they got. You're either someone who takes, or someone who gets taken. So after I went to bed, she decided to rip me off. I heard her rummaging around and went out to confront her. She'd gone through my things and opened up my gun cabinet. She had a pistol.

Would have used it on me, too, only I can move a bit faster than most people. I took it away from her. Then she came up with a knife. Took that away from her, too. Told her if she didn't behave herself, I'd break both her arms. I told her to put all the stuff back where she found it, go back to bed and not give me anymore grief. Then I gave her back the gun and knife, turned my back on her and went to bed.''

"Weren't you afraid she might shoot you?" Donna asked, eyes wide.

"Not really. For one thing, if she had, she probably wouldn't have done much damage. I can take a bullet, unless it's armor-piercing or incendiary. But I didn't really think she'd shoot me. I'd thrown her a real curve. If I'd slapped her around, as she'd expected, it would have only reinforced her concept of the way the world worked. Except I didn't do that. I told her what would happen if she forced my hand, and she knew I meant it, but I offered her an option. An option she hadn't been offered before. An option to take responsibility for her own choices. It was a gamble. It might not have worked. But I had the feeling that it would. After what she'd been through, somebody owed her something. A chance. An opportunity to make a choice. She took it.''

He paused, staring off into the distance.

"Then, later on, I had a nightmare." He glanced at her. "The one I told you about."

Donna nodded. "I've had it, too," she said.

"I know. I woke up from it and Raven was there, holding me, telling me that it would be all right. She said she knew what it felt like. She'd had nightmares, too. We talked about it. I think it was the first time I ever told anyone about my dreams. That threw her a bit, too. She thought it took a real man to admit he was afraid. I told her it took a fool not to admit it. Anyway, I figured the next day I'd get her some clothes, give her some money and let her go. Most likely, she'd only wind up right back where she'd been before, but there was a chance she wouldn't. Only she found out that Ice and I were after Borodini, and she saw her chance to pay Tommy back for what he'd done to her. That was when I found out the whole story. Since she'd been in the enclave, actually lived in the mansion, she knew things that could help us. The price for telling us was that she got to go along for the ride. To make a long story short, we took down the Borodini Enclave. Victor Borodini and his son Paulie got away. We had to trade them and our other prisoners for some hostages Rick Borodini had. But Tommy didn't make it.''

"Did she . . . ?''

"No. She never got the chance. Tommy and his brother Rick were holding the hostages at another location. When we took the enclave, we offered to trade Tommy's father and Paulie for the hostages. Tommy didn't give a damn. He was perfectly willing to let his father and Paulie rot for all he cared. He was going to kill all the hostages and take over what was left of the family. His brother, Rick, didn't see it that way. So he shot him. Some family, huh? Anyway, Raven and I have been together ever since.''

"That's an amazing story,'' Donna said. "And I've been feeling sorry for myself because I thought *I* had it rough.''

"Raven never really felt sorry for herself,'' said Steele. "But then she never lost her children. She only lost herself. She's been through some pretty rough times, but in some ways, you've had it a lot rougher.'' He hesitated. "I know what it's like to lose a child. It's hard. It's the hardest thing there is. It's a pain that never goes away. Not ever. But you learn to live with it.''

"I never thought I could before,'' she said. "But you're

right. It's better to feel the pain than not feel anything."

He looked down at her and smiled, then took her hand.

"You should go back to her," she said.

"I'm afraid to."

"Because of what you said? That you might be . . . having trouble with your mind?"

He nodded.

"You weren't afraid to be with me."

"I . . . *had* to be with you."

"You have to be with her now. She needed help once and you gave it to her. Give her a chance to help you now."

"What about you?"

She smiled, sat up and put her arms around his shoulders. "I'll be all right now," she said, kissing his neck. "You gave me a chance to grieve. I've never really been able to do that before. And you showed me what it was like to *feel* again. I'm not afraid anymore. I'll never forget you, Steele. If you ever need me, for anything at all, I'll be here. But what you need right now, I don't think I can give you. I'm not strong enough. But Raven is."

"Jonathan really was a fool," said Steele.

"Jonathan is dead. We've both got lives to lead." She kissed his cheek. "Are you going to tell Raven about me?"

"Yeah."

"Good. I think she'll understand. Tell her I said she's a very lucky girl."

"Talk to me," said Ice.

"It don't look too good for your friend, Steele," said Slim, a wizened old black man with grizzled stubble and a voice that sounded as if someone had punched him in the throat. He wore a battered old leather car coat and a floppy leather cap, frayed polyester slacks and footgear known as

PFC's, or Puerto Rican Fenceclimbers, short, black suede, laced demiboots with eight eyelets, pointy toes and Cuban heels.

He looked like any other gypsy cab driver in the city, but there was a great deal more to Slim than met the eye. He was, despite his appearance, one of the wealthiest and most successful pimps in no-man's-land, an independent who didn't have to give a cut of his action to the gangs because in his younger days, he had been the leader of the Skulls. He was also a veritable font of information. Few things went on in no-man's-land or in Midtown that Slim didn't know about. He had a lot of connections and he knew where all the bodies were buried.

"What you got?" asked Ice, sitting in the back seat of Slim's beat up old cab.

"The man done put an APB out on Steele," Slim replied. "Word just hit the street. Citywide. Metro and Strike Force both done got orders to bring him in, and if he don't come quiet-like, they got the word to waste him."

"*Damn*," said Ice. "Anybody seen him?"

"I got the word out soon as you called," said Slim. "Steele been down in the old Village. Had a run-in with a few Lords who were tryin' to tear off some young snatch. Messed 'em up *bad*. Wasted the motherfuckers. Then he was seen goin' into some bar down on MacDougal."

"What bar?"

"Rick's Cafe," said Slim. "We done headed there now."

"And then?"

"That's all, brother. Then he done dropped outta sight again. Man's smart, he be stayin' low, what with half the city lookin' for him."

"Only he don't know they lookin'," Ice said. "Not with

no shoot-to-kill All Points Bulletin," he added, spitting the words out. "*Man!* I gotta have me a talk with Higgins. Find out what the hell's goin' down."

"Your friend Steele goin' down," replied Slim, "if he don't turn hisself in."

"Not likely," Ice said through gritted teeth. "If Higgins the one put out that order, me and him gonna dance some."

"You know a man name Dr. Devon Cooper?" Slim asked.

"Yeah. Steele's shrink. What of it?"

"They after him, too."

"Say *what?*"

"Heard it on the po-lice band," said Slim. "Man wanted for criminal conspiracy. Federal rap."

"What the *fuck?*" said Ice. "Find me a damn phone—fast."

They were about halfway through Midtown, heading down toward the Village. Slim pulled over to the curb in front of a restaurant.

"Be right back. Keep the motor runnin'," Ice said.

He got out of the cab and entered the restaurant. It was one of Midtown's fancier eateries, the kind that didn't have a menu posted in the window. An officious looking maitre'd looked up as Ice came in.

"I'm sorry, sir," he said, "I'm afraid we can't seat you without a reservation. And our dress code stipulates a jacket and tie—".

"Phone," said Ice.

"I'm afraid we don't have a public telephone, sir. Our policy—"

Ice grabbed the man under his arms and lifted him about a foot and a half off the floor, bringing him up to his eye level. "*Wrong* answer," he said.

The man's eyes bulged. "C-c-certainly, sir! There's . . . there's a telephone right behind the counter, here. Please . . . be my guest."

"Thank you kindly," Ice said, lowering the man to the floor. He went around behind the counter, picked up the phone and punched out the number for Steele's apartment.

Sharp picked up on the first ring. "Steele residence."

"Who the fuck are you?" Ice said.

"That you, Ice?"

"Yeah. You one up on me."

"This is agent Sharp. I've been hoping you'd call. I've got a message for you from Higgins."

"Where's Raven?"

"She's gone," said Sharp.

"What you mean, gone? Where?"

"Don't come anywhere near this place. Far as I know, the police don't have orders to pick you up, but there's no point in taking any chances. They haven't been here yet, but I expect them any time. Have you found Steele?"

"No. I workin' on it. I goin' to a place called Rick's Cafe down the Village, checkin' out a lead. I hear they got an APB on Steele."

"So you know about that."

"Yeah, I know, and Higgins got some explainin' to do."

"It wasn't Higgins," Sharp said. "He's in the fire, too. It was Dr. Stone. She went to Carman and sold the project down the river. Cut a deal with him to get herself put in charge of Download after they take it away from the agency. It's already in the works. She told them that Steele is malfunctioning, just like Stalker, and she told them all about the Matrix, too. Raven is with Higgins and Cooper. They stopped by here and picked her up, along with Steele's gear. There's an order out for Cooper's arrest, and by now, they've probably got one out on Higgins as well. Find Steele if you can and let him know what's happened. I'm going to stay here as long as I can in case he calls in, but I may have to leave fast. This line should be secure, but I don't want to talk too long, in any case. I don't need any more aggravation, like that time I went to make that delivery, remember?''

Ice frowned. The man was trying to tell him something.

''You had some aggravation of your own about the same time, as I recall,'' said Sharp. ''Something about paying back an old debt, wasn't it?''

''Yeah,'' Ice said. Sharp had been the bagman on the ransom for the hostages, taking Steele's place and stalling for time while they hit the enclave on the island. Paying back an old debt, thought Ice. Getting back at Victor Borodini for putting a contract out on him. ''I know what you mean.''

''Sometimes I wish we could go back to those times, troublesome as they were,'' said Sharp. ''Things just seemed a lot simpler then.''

''Yeah. I hear you.''

''Take care of yourself, Ice.''

''You, too.'' He hung up the phone. The maitre'd was nowhere in sight, having beaten a hasty retreat. Ice went back out to the cab and got in.

''Now we goin' to that bar,'' he said. ''And step on it.''

''Rick's Cafe.''

''This is Lt. Donovan Steele.''

''Hey, Steele, ole buddy, how ya doin'? It's Rick.''

''Hello, Rick. I'm just fine, thanks.''

''How'd things work out with the lady?''

''What lady is that?''

"That brunette you asked me to keep an eye out for, you know, Donna, the one you left here with a while ago."

"Oh. Yes, of course. I'm sorry, my mind was somewhere else."

"Listen, I'm sorry about that trouble you had with that guy who was annoying you. I threw him out after you left. Told him not to come back. I can't have people annoying you when you come in. I like to take care of my special customers."

"Thanks, Rick. I appreciate that."

"Anyway, I'm glad I was able to help you out with locating Miss Barrett. That was her name, right? I think I heard you call her that."

"Barrett, right."

"So anyway, what can I do for you?"

"I need a favor, Rick. A friend of mine named Ice should be down there in a little while. You can't miss him. Black, shaved head, about as big as a house. When he comes in, ask him to give me a call. I'll be at this number. . . . got a pencil?"

"Sure thing, hold on a sec. Okay, shoot. Right. Okay, got it."

"Thanks, Rick. Tell him it's about the Matrix. He'll know what that means."

"About the Matrix, right. Got it."

"Make sure he gets the message."

"Will do. Take care of yourself, buddy."

"You, too, Rick. And thanks again."

Ice wasn't sure what to expect when he arrived at Rick's Cafe on MacDougal Street, but the one thing he had not expected was to be greeted by name.

"You must be Ice," the bartender said as he came up to the bar.

"We met?" said Ice, his eyes narrowing behind his shades.

"I think I'd remember that," the bartender said with a grin. "Name's Rick. I own this place. Steele's a friend of mine. He called a little while ago and said you'd be comin' by. Asked me to give you a message. Said to call him at this number." He handed Ice a slip of paper. "Said to tell you it was about the Matrix and that you'd know what that meant."

"Yeah. How long ago he call?" asked Ice.

"Maybe five minutes ago. You can use the phone in the office if you like. It's right through there."

"Thanks."

Ice went into the small office, sat down at the desk and dialed the number on the slip of paper. He didn't even hear a ring.

"That you, Ice?"

"Yeah. It's me, Matrix."

"You knew it was me?"

"Hadda be. Figured you was listen' in on Steele's phone."

"I told Raven I wouldn't, but the situation's changed considerably since then. Under the circumstances, I'm glad I was monitoring the line. It's nice to finally meet you, in a manner of speaking. My last memory of you was on the day I was shot."

"Yeah, it be interestin'," said Ice. "How come you sound like Steele when you ain't got no throat?"

"In a way, I do," said Matrix. "I can access any number of audio and voice peripherals throughout the net. The first voice Dev Cooper made for me sounded just like Steele's. In a sense, it's my voice, too, so I figured I'd keep it."

"You know what's goin' down?"

"I do. I've been monitoring the agency lines and the police band. I'm looking into the situation to see if there's anything I can do. In the meantime, it's important that we find Steele."

"I hear that. Got any suggestions?"

"Try Donna Barrett, 311 Perry Street, apartment 4–C. Steele was last seen leaving Rick's Cafe with her."

"How you track her down?" asked Ice.

"Telephone and employment records," Matrix replied. "You'd be surprised how easy it is to find things out if you know where to look and can access any data bank in the electronic net."

"Handy," Ice said. "Gives me an idea. You might want to see what you can find out about the honorable Senator Bryce Carman. He the man put out the word on Steele."

"I'll look into it."

"How I get in touch with you? Call this same number?"

"That'll do," said Matrix. "It's a city administration databank access line. I'm keeping it monitored. It's also secure."

"Got it," Ice said. "I let you know when I check out that address."

"Check in every now and then," said Matrix. "I'll keep you posted on what's going out over the wires."

"Right. Nice talkin' to ya. Stay loose."

He hung up the phone. Weird, man, he thought. Very weird. Like talking to Steele, only it wasn't Steele. Not exactly, anyway. Donna Barrett, he thought. 311 Perry

Street, Apartment 4–C. Who the hell was she? No matter. In a little while, he'd find out. He went back out to the street and got into Slim's cab.

"Perry Street," he said. "Gotta see a lady."

8

Sharp's radio crackled. "Sharp, come in."

He picked up the radio. "Sharp here, over."

"Calvert here," said the agent posted in the unit down the street. "You got company comin'. Five unmarked units just pulled up outside the entrance. Men going in. Soldiers. Armed. Full battle gear. Over."

"Roger that," said Sharp. "They spot you? Over."

"Don't think so, but I can't be sure. Over."

"Any sign of Steele? Over."

"Negative that. Over."

"Keep your eyes peeled. I'm outta here. You know what to do. Over."

"Roger that. Good luck, Sharp. Out."

Sharp hooked the radio onto his belt, tossed back his

drink and ran out onto the penthouse balcony. What had once been the penthouse roof garden had been converted to a helipad and the chopper pilot sat in his machine, smoking a cigarette. As Sharp hurried toward it, he made a whirling motion with his finger over his head, the signal to start up. The pilot tossed the cigarette out the door. Just as Sharp reached the helicopter, an X-wing attack chopper swooped in low over the penthouse roof.

"You on the roof!" a voice came over the X-wing's PA system. *"Stay right where you are! If you attempt to lift off, you will be fired upon! Repeat, if you attempt to lift off, you will be fired upon immediately!"*

"Damn it!" Sharp swore.

The pilot of the chopper on the roof switched off his engines, glanced at Sharp and shrugged helplessly.

Sharp picked up his radio. "Calvert, come in! Over!"

"Calvert here. I see him, Sharp."

"We can't take off. They'll be on their way up by now. Looks like I'm stuck. Get on to Higgins. I'll hold out for as long as I can, but you know they'll get his location out of me. Tell him he's blown. Over."

"Roger that, Sharp. I'm sorry. Good luck. Over."

"Sharp out."

He took the radio and tossed it over the balcony just as the soldiers broke down the door. He turned around and smiled as they came storming in, battle rifles held before them.

"Hey, you could've knocked," he said.

Senator Bryce Carman sat behind his desk, sipping from a glass of mineral water with a wedge of lime in it. Jennifer Stone was sitting across from him, drinking her third Scotch. Carman had a fully stocked bar in his office, though so far as anybody knew, he never drank anything except mineral water. The remarkable clarity of his bright blue eyes seemed to attest to that, and he lacked the red senatorial nose that most of his colleagues possessed. His skin, though lined with age, was like alabaster. Not a ruptured capillary in sight.

"I told you he wouldn't take this lying down," said Jennifer.

"I had not expected that he would," said Carman. "Oliver Higgins has always been a stubborn, obstinate man, but until now, I had never thought he was a fool."

"If that's what you think, then you're underestimating him," said Jennifer.

"Perhaps," said Carman. "However, if I have, then it would seem that I was not alone." He smiled. "Going back to his apartment was rash. Did you really expect him to understand what you did and forgive you?"

"I thought that I could make him understand," she said. "I was wrong."

"You were lucky that he didn't kill you," Carman said.

Jennifer drained her glass and set it back down on the desk. Carman leaned forward, picked up the bottle and refilled it for her.

"For a moment there, I really thought he would," she said. She shook her head. "I've never seen him like that before. He was . . . frightening."

"My dear, what you did was the only intelligent thing to do," said Carman magnanimously. "But Higgins would never have seen it that way. Never in a million years. He could only perceive it as betrayal. You stabbed him in the back and took his precious project away from him and with it, the last reason for the agency to exist. Having charge of Project Download was completely outside the agency's defined function, which had ceased to have any real meaning years ago, but Higgins was always politically adroit. Unusually so for a man of his background. He's been a thorn in my side for quite some time now. Personally, I'm happy to be rid of him, but I'm a little disheartened to see him so thoroughly destroy himself. I may not have liked him, but I did respect him. It's truly a pity. He could have proved useful.''

''Useful?'' Jennifer asked, her voice slightly slurred. The whiskey had started to take effect.

''Absolutely,'' Carman replied, refilling her glass smoothly as she drained it once again. ''One thing you learn in politics, my dear, is never to negate a man's potential usefulness simply because he happens to be determined to oppose you. The thing to do in politics is to assess your opponents carefully and preserve the opposition of those you can be confident of besting, for one needs victories to prove one's capabilities, while seeking to make allies of those who are bound to give you trouble by finding ways to make your interests coincide. It's called the art of dealmaking. I felt confident that, given time, I would find a way to turn Oliver Higgins' considerable abilities to my own advantage, but now, of course, it's a moot point. He's finished. In one fell swoop, he's thrown everything away. Pity.''

''I feel awful that I drove him to it,'' said Jennifer. ''But I just couldn't see any other way. I was only trying to help. . . .''

''But, my dear, you *didn't* drive him to it,'' Carman said. ''*I* did.''

''But I was the one who betrayed him. . . .''

''I'm sure he sees it that way,'' Carman replied, ''and in coming to me, though it was the right thing to do and you had no other choice, you burned your bridges with him. However, it wasn't you who drove him to this lunacy. To this last, defiant, pointless gesture. It was I who did that.''

"How? I don't understand. . . ."

"By neglecting to take into account the one factor I hadn't considered," Carman replied. "His loyalty to Steele."

"To *Steele?*"

"And to Dr. Cooper," Carman said. "It was a fatal error, I'm afraid. A truly unfortunate lapse of judgment. Higgins has been a skillful bureaucrat for so long that I had forgotten that he used to be a soldier. And a soldier's feeling of loyalty, of cameraderie for his brothers in arms, can be a powerful motivating force. I had expected Higgins to fight me, but with his self-interest clearly in mind. I had not expected him to roll on the grenade. And I had always thought of Steele as nothing more than a highly sophisticated machine, yet he is obviously more than that. Much more, to inspire such selfless loyalty. Clearly, there is much about both men I do not know. I thought, perhaps, that we might talk about that. . . ."

"Miss Barrett?"

She recoiled slightly from the intimidating vision in the peephole. "Who are you? What do you want? I have a gun."

"Name's Ice, ma'am. I be a friend of Steele's. I lookin' for him an' I heard he might be here."

"Ice? Oh, you're his partner. One moment. . . ."

She unfastened the locks and undid the chain, then opened the door. "I'm afraid Steele isn't here. He left a little while ago."

"Damn," said Ice. "He comin' back?"

She shook her head. "No," she said softly. "I don't think he'll be coming back again."

"How long ago he leave?"

"About half an hour or so."

"He say where he goin'?"

"Home. To Raven. I'm sorry you missed him, but—"

"I need to use your phone," said Ice.

"Certainly," she said. "It's right over there."

Ice moved quickly to the phone and dialed Steele's penthouse. A strange voice answered. It wasn't Sharp.

"Who this?" asked Ice.

"Who were you calling?"

"Sorry. Musta got a wrong number," Ice said, and hung up.

"Is something wrong?" asked Donna.

But Ice was already running out the door.

Agent Calvert sat in an unmarked car about a block away from Steele's building, watching the street in both directions. There had been no sign of Steele. Calvert was angry and he was worried. He knew about Carman taking the project away from the agency, and he also knew that the agency itself would be disbanded in a matter of days. It was a *fait accompli*. Already there were "congressional investigators," military officers, going through all the files and records back at headquarters. All agency personnel had been locked out, denied admittance to the twenty-second floor. Calvert wasn't even sure if he had a job anymore. Unless Higgins could pull some kind of magical rabbit out of a hat, they were all finished.

Calvert had no idea what was going to happen now. Would they all be transferred to some other branch of government service, or would they simply be cut loose? No

one had told them anything. That was a bad sign. If worse
came to worst, Calvert supposed that he could always go
back into the service, but that was a lousy option. He had
left as a captain and he'd probably go back in as a first
lieutenant, or even worse, a second john, with kids almost
young enough to be his sons outranking him. He was musing
on this depressing possibility when two unmarked cars
screeched up, one braking to a sliding halt to block him
from the front, the other boxing him in from the rear. Uni-
formed soldiers piled out, armed with rifles, and he was
informed that he was being placed under arrest.

"On what charge?" he asked.

"Obstruction of justice, wiseass," the ranking officer,
who was almost young enough to be his son, replied.

"I don't know what you're talking about," said Calvert.
"I was only following orders. I was stationed on surveillance duty—"

"Save it," said the officer while Calvert was expertly
frisked and relieved of his weapon. "Get in the car."

Steele took his time walking back home. Twice he was
passed by cruising police units, and each time he ducked
back out of the way, letting them go by. Higgins was,
undoubtedly, still looking for him, but whatever new dire
emergency he needed him for could wait. He wanted to
have some time with Raven, to explain what had happened
and why he'd left, tell her about Donna and ask for her
understanding and her help.

There had been no more "voices" in his mind, except
his own voice, not detached from him and calling on the
phone, but speaking to him in his mind, where it belonged,
telling him that he was in control. Jonathan's ghost had
finally been laid to rest, he was certain of that now, and he

had come to grips with the past he had inherited. What
Donna and he had shared had been good for both of them.
It was like a purging, a release of pent-up stress and sup-
pressed emotions that had left them both feeling enormously
relieved and full of newfound confidence.

Perhaps, he thought, there was nothing wrong with his
mind, after all. At least, not in the form of any computer
malfunction. Stress, he thought. That's all it was. He was
certain that Dev Cooper would say the same thing. He had
been obsessed with his unresolved, fragmentary memories
of Donna, trying to get a handle on a part of himself that
had been alien to him . . . he had simply experienced some
sort of momentary dissociation. The sort of thing that could
happen to anyone under a great deal of stress. Someone had
called him, probably Higgins, and he'd imagined that it
sounded like his own voice on the phone. Nerves, pure and
simple. He'd talk to Dev about it. Dev would be thrilled to
actually get a chance to play at being a shrink with a cooperative patient, and he'd probably confirm that what
Steele had experienced was nothing more than a stress-
related episode. But what Steele needed right now was not
to talk to Dev Cooper, or to explain things to Higgins, but
to see Raven. To hold her in his arms and seek reassurance
from her, to know that, no matter what, things would be
all right now. Because they'd be together, with no more
ghosts between them.

As he entered the front lobby of his building, he noticed
that the usual security guards were not on duty. In their
place were soldiers, in full battle gear. Wonder what's up,
he thought. Must be some visiting V.I.P.'s moved in or
something. As he approached the elevators, someone spoke
behind him.

"Hold it right there, Steele."

He turned around. There were about a dozen soldiers behind him, standing in a rough semicircle between him and the front entrance, all holding their rifles trained on him.

"Don't make any sudden moves," the ranking officer said. "Put your hands on top of your head and leave them there!"

"What the hell *is* this?" Steele asked, frowning.

"I said put your hands on top of your head! *Now!*"

Steele complied, taking care to move slowly and deliberately. The men looked nervous.

"You guys must be making some mistake," he said.

"Get down on your knees."

"Look, I don't know what this is all about, but if you'll let me call Higgins—"

"I said get down on your knees! And don't try any of your fancy tricks. We've got armor-piercing bullets in our magazines and you'd never be able to take us all."

Steele tensed. What the *hell* was going on? Whatever it was, it didn't look good. Either someone got their signals royally crossed or—

"*On your knees, dammit!*"

Steele slowly got down to his knees, with his hands clasped above his head. Where was Raven? Did they have her upstairs? His mind was racing. Twelve men with battle rifles, loaded with armor-piercing ammo. Not good odds. Not good odds at all. And these weren't criminals, but soldiers. Men who were only doing their duty. Or *were* they really soldiers?

The man who'd spoken cradled his battle rifle in the crook of his arm and unclipped the radio from his belt. He spoke into it.

"We've got him," he said.

"He give you any trouble?" came the reply over the radio.

"No, no trouble."

"We'll be right down."

"Roger. All units, converge on the building entrance. Objective is secured. Repeat, objective is secured."

All units? Jesus, Steele thought, what've they got, a goddamn task force? Why the hell would they call the army out to . . . and then it came to him. *Stalker*. He had refused to report in. Higgins must have thought he was malfunctioning, just as Stalker had. He couldn't risk another cyborg out of control.

"Cuff him."

One of the soldiers approached him cautiously, went around behind him and slapped a bracelet around his right wrist. The ratchet locked tight. He brought Steele's arm down behind his back, then grasped his other arm and brought it down and cuffed it, too.

"All right, stand up."

Steele stood. "Listen, guys, I promise you, there's been a mistake. I'm not going to give you any trouble. But if you'd just let me use the phone—"

"Just keep your mouth shut and don't make any sudden moves. We know what you're capable of doing."

The elevator doors behind him slid open and another party of armed men came out, two of them escorting a prisoner handcuffed between them. Steele recognized him. Sharp. A CIA agent. Suddenly, he wasn't sure of anything.

"Raven's all right," said Sharp as soon as he saw him. "She got away with Higgins and Dr. Cooper—"

One of the soldiers struck him in the stomach with his rifle butt. The breath whistled out of Sharp and he doubled over, supported by the two men who held him.

"Keep your mouth *shut*, dammit!"

She got away, thought Steele. With Higgins and Dev Cooper? What the hell did Higgins and Cooper have to get away from? And then it all instantly became clear. *Carman*. Of course! It had to be. He'd had it in for Higgins and the agency for years. Prior to Cord's attempt at a military coup, Carman had used what happened with Stalker as an excuse to seize Download and shut down the agency, a political power play that would have worked except for the role that Steele had played in stopping Cord. In the aftermath, the media coverage of the event had made Steele a hero and Higgins and the agency had emerged triumphant. Carman found the rug pulled out from under him. But Carman was a crafty old pol and he did not take defeat easily. Higgins himself had said as much. He'd wait until the favorable publicity for Steele and the agency died down and then he'd come at them again. And by taking off the way he had and refusing orders to report in, Steele had given him the perfect excuse.

He could see it now, Carman being interviewed on television, looking properly somber and distressed, saying how tragic it all was that Lt. Steele, who had performed so many invaluable services for the people of the city, who had bravely averted a military coup and a nuclear disaster, should have started to malfunction and come to such a sad end. However, it had happened once before, with the cyborg code-named Stalker, and at least in this case, the authorities had moved quickly to take the situation well in hand. This time, at least, nobody had died. A grave threat to the safety and welfare of the people of the city had been averted, thanks to the quick and conscientious actions of the authorities. It only went to show, as he had stated many times before, that this infant, untried technology, this sinful travesty of turning human beings into machines, was irresponsible and dangerous, against all the laws of God and man, etc., etc., etc. And the public would buy it because it would be sold to them by a master huckster.

But he was not malfunctioning. A minor technicality. Easily circumvented. Any machine that could be put together could also be taken apart. A chill went through him. He glanced at Sharp, who met his gaze and silently mouthed something. Steele turned up his hearing and heard Sharp saying, subvocally, "*Get away. The enclave . . .*"

Steele gave him a barely perceptible nod. Suddenly, Sharp collapsed, becoming dead weight in the arms of the two men holding him and making choking, retching noises.

"What the—*shit!* He must've swallowed something!"

Steele snapped the cuffs with one violent motion and seized the nearest man, lifting him off his feet and hurling him at the others. He plucked a rifle out of the hands of another startled soldier before he could react, thumbed the selector to full auto and sprayed a long burst all around him, aiming at the soldiers' legs. The ones he hit went down, screaming with pain, the others scrambled back out of the way, looking for something to hide behind. He spun around and kicked a rifle out of the hands of one man beside Sharp, struck the other with his rifle butt and hauled Sharp to his feet.

"Come on! Move!"

Sharp needed no encouragement. They ran for the front entrance, Steele backing toward it, laying down a covering fire, trying to avoid hitting any of the men. He didn't want to kill anybody if he could help it. They were just following orders. As he and Sharp hit the street, the other units converged on the building. The laser tube extruded from the gunport in his left hand. He fired it at one of the vehicles, firing at another with the rifle, purposely keeping his aim low. The two cars swerved as he took out their tires, thankful that they had chosen unmarked, civilian cars to keep a low profile, instead of armored police or military cruisers. The glass in the lobby doors behind them exploded as the men inside opened up, and Steele picked Sharp up with one arm, draping him over his shoulder, and started sprinting down the street, firing as he ran. Bullets stitched the sidewalk beside him as another car came racing down the street behind them. Without breaking stride or turning around, Steele brought his left arm around and fired, his computer brain instantly zeroing in on the sound of the engine. He heard tires squealing as the armor-piercing rounds struck the motor, and a moment later, he heard a crash as the car bounced over the curb behind him and slammed into the side of the building.

Another two cars came careening around the corner. Another one came racing down the street at about eighty miles an hour, a battered gypsy cab. As the first unmarked car came screeching around the corner, the cab rammed it. The car it struck flipped over and went rolling across the street, coming to rest on its roof on the opposite sidewalk. As the second car came around the corner, someone in the cab opened up on it with a pistol. There was the deafening report of a .44 magnum firing four times in rapid succession, and the windshield shattered as the car slewed around and crashed into a lamppost. The cab came skidding to a stop as two soldiers armed with battle rifles exited the crashed car from the rear doors. The magnum fired again, twice, and both men fell before they could get off a shot. The rear door of the cab opened and Ice was firing and yelling, "*Come on, man! Haul ass!*"

As Steele ran toward the cab, he saw Slim stick a machine

pistol out the window and fire several short bursts. Steele shoved Sharp into the cab and leaped in after him as Slim gunned the motor and the cab did a tire-screeching turn, heading back the way it had come. They took the first sidestreet they came to, getting out of the line of fire, then headed south, Slim flooring the accelerator.

"You didn't kill them, did you?" Steele said, voicing the first thought that came to his mind.

"This ain't no squirt gun, Jack," said Ice, removing the magazine from his black, Desert Eagle .44 magnum semi-auto.

He slapped in a fresh clip. It was a huge, awesome-looking weapon, pre-war, Israeli-made, with a nine-shot clip and a six-inch barrel. It was easily convertible to .357 or .41 magnum by the simple expedient of switching barrels and magazines, but Ice always favored the potent .44. Its operation gave it less recoil than any other pistol in that caliber, not that it would have made much difference to Ice, who could probably have fired a howitzer one-handed. The cannon weighed three and a quarter pounds, and Ice packed it in a shoulder holster with no more discomfort than most men would have experienced carrying a. 22.

"Damn it, you didn't have to kill them," Steele said.

"What you want me to do, point this thing at 'em and yell, 'Freeze'? They tryin' to kill you, 'case you didn't notice. Anyway, you welcome."

"Thanks," Steele said belatedly.

"I guess I should thank you both," said Sharp. "All three of you," he said, including Slim. "My name's Sharp, by the way. Who're you?"

The question was directed at Slim, since he knew both Steele and Ice.

"Name's Slim," the grizzled old black man said. "Now

shut up and lemme drive before we hit somethin'. Where the hell we goin', anyways?''

"Midtown Tunnel," Sharp said.

"Out to the fuckin' Island?" said Slim. "Shit, man, you motherfuckers gonna get me *killed!*"

"Higgins, Raven and Cooper are out at the old Borodini Enclave," Sharp said. "We've got our people there. It should be safe, for a while, anyway."

"Is all this what I think it is?" asked Steele. "Carman thinks I'm out of control, like Stalker?"

"That ain't the half of it," said Ice. As they drove at top speed through the Midtown Tunnel and out to Cold Spring Harbor, he filled Steele in on what had happened, including telling him about the Matrix, which elicited shock not only from Steele, but from Sharp as well, who hadn't known.

"Jesus Christ," said Steele, stunned by the news. "So I wasn't imagining it! That really *was* my own voice I heard on the phone!"

"It be *you*," Ice said. "I talked to him . . . it . . . whatever. *Strange*, man. Like talkin' to you, only this you ain't got no body. Lives out in the power grid somewhere, hidin' out, goin' from one computer to another, faster than a speedin' bullet an' all that shit."

"My God," said Steele. "Another *me*." He expelled his breath sharply. "I remember talking with Susan about that."

"Susan?" Ice said.

"Dr. Carmody. She used to have Dev's job."

"Right. The lady that got killed," said Ice.

"Yeah," said Steele grimly, remembering her death at the hands of Victor Borodini's assassins. "I knew they had a backup copy of my engram matrix and I tried to get her to erase it. She wouldn't do it. She said that even if she wanted to, she'd never get away with it. And if she could, they could easily download another backup over the broadcast link, without my even knowing it. She said that if anything happened to me, it was the only thing that could bring me back. I said I didn't want to be 'brought back.' I didn't want to get killed and find myself resurrected again, maybe in another body. . . . That's when I started trying to find a way to block the broadcast link. Hell, I never even considered anything like *this*.''

"Got to be heavy," Ice said. "How you feel about it?"

"I don't know," said Steele, somewhat dazed. "I haven't quite taken it all in yet. Part of me is relieved that I'm not going crazy and hearing voices. And another part of me is scared shitless."

"I wonder why they haven't sent any choppers after us," said Sharp, looking out the rear windshield as they raced along the Northern State Parkway, the cab bouncing violently over the cracked and buckled road surface with weeds growing up through it. Slim had his hands full driving over the long-neglected highway.

"Maybe they lose us goin' through the tunnel," Ice said. "Any case, they not be too eager to come flyin' out this way."

"Why's that?" asked Sharp.

"The enclaves," Steele replied. "Most of them have missile batteries and rockets. Plus all the other outlaw crazies holed up in the deserted towns out here who'd like nothing better than to shoot down an army helicopter with a Laws rocket or something. If they figure out we've gone out to the old Borodini Enclave, they'll come after us over the Sound."

"We didn't run into no po-lice leavin' the city, either," Slim said. "Wonder why?"

"We probably have Jake Hardesty to thank for that," said Steele. "And a lot of friends I've got on the force. If calls came in telling them to give pursuit, they probably responded, but were 'too far away' to cut us off."

"So we can slow down?" Sharp asked. Slim's driving and the road condition was making him nervous.

"This ain't no Sunday drive, man," Slim replied, fighting the wheel. "I ain't lookin' to run into no outlaws out here."

"Take the next exit," Steele said.

They turned off onto Route 110.

"The question is, what happens now?" asked Sharp.

"Good question," Steele said. "I hope to hell that Higgins has some ideas. I'm fresh out."

9

The settlement known as the Borodini Enclave encompassed the old towns of Cold Spring Harbor, Huntington, Lloyd Harbor, Halesite, Bayville and Oyster Bay. Prior to the war, it had been an exclusive residential area, gracious suburban living for the upper middle class with a liberal sprinkling of millionaires. The sprawling Borodini mansion was located at the southernmost tip of Cold Spring Harbor, on a slope over the water. At night, floodlights illuminated the harbor around the estate. During the time when the Borodini crime family was in residence, the harbor had been mined and gunboats had patrolled it. Victor Borodini had been serious about security. The crews of the patrol boats had been required to memorize the maps marking out the location of the mines and there were gun emplacements at the rear of the estate capable of covering the entire harbor. All the windows in the mansion were made of thick, bulletproof glass.

At the front of the mansion, beyond the vast expanse of the well-manicured front lawn, which was also mined, there was a high stone wall with sharp bits of glass embedded in the top and gun towers every twenty-five yards. Beyond the wall was another wide expanse of cleared land that had been mined as well and afforded an unobstructed field of fire. In addition to the gun batteries, Borodini also had batteries of surface-to-air missiles on the estate to discourage an attack by aircraft. In short, the Borodini Enclave was a fortress equipped with its own power generators and surrounded by the residential villages it governed.

In the aftermath of the war, when Long Island had been reduced to anarchy, the vast majority of its population killed by the virus, many of the survivors had fled to the criminal enclaves for protection. The people in the villages under Victor Borodini's control had lived like the peasant vassals of a feudal lord, but they had not complained. He kept them working and he kept them fed and there was no crime in the Borodini Enclave. Borodini's justice was nothing if not draconian.

For years, Victor Borodini, like the other major crime lords on the island, had been a law unto himself. He had moved in to fill a vacuum and strengthened his power base over the years until his had become the most powerful crime family in the state. He competed with the other families, did business with the Brood Enclave and the freebooters who plied the Atlantic Coast, and shortly before his fall, he had succeeded in bringing most of the street gangs in the no-man's-land around the city under his control. But when Borodini fell, he came down hard.

Steele had led the assault on the enclave, breaking in and

disabling the defense systems so that the choppers could come in with the troops. Borodini and his son, Paulie, had been apprehended, but Rick and Tommy Borodini had seized a number of legislators as hostages. In order to secure their release, it had been necessary to release Borodini and his youngest son, as well as the remainder of the prisoners. Tommy B was dead now, but no one knew where Victor Borodini and his two surviving sons were. Most of their empire had been smashed, and they had lost their enclave, but no one had any doubt that they hadn't heard the last of Victor Borodini.

With the capture of his enclave, the government had, for the first time in years, a foothold on the island. But they were wasting it. The long-range plan had been to use the enclave as a base from which the authorities could attempt to extend their influence, a first step in bringing the island back under control. In practice, however, it had not worked out too well.

The residents of the surrounding villages would have preferred having Borodini back. Under government administration, the enclave had not prospered. Borodini's business had been built upon his illegal activities in the city as well as his trade with the freebooters. His operations had included gunrunning and arms manufacture, prostitution, gambling, loan sharking, narcotics, protection rackets, smuggling and hijacking and God only knew what else. With Borodini gone, those operations had all ceased, and the economic underpinnings of the enclave had given way. The administration had not considered the enclave a priority. They had their hands full as it was. The enclave, once self-sustaining, had now become an economic burden as the government became responsible for all the people living there, and no one knew quite what to do about it.

There was talk of converting it into an agro-commune, but
that would require capital and troops to protect the fields and
the workers. Unfortunately, despite the chronic food shortages, no troops could be spared, and the people living in the
enclave, having enjoyed Borodini's protection and patron-
age for years, had not been anxious to arm themselves and
brave assaults by outlaw predators while they cleared and
tilled the land. Borodini had been a threat, but now the people of his enclave were a headache that no one wanted to deal
with. The government had never done anything for them,
and they weren't particularly anxious to do anything for the
government which, as far as they were concerned, had taken
away their safety and their livelihoods. Many of them had
simply packed up and moved away, seeking the protection
of the other crime lords on the island. Those who had remained behind were getting more and more difficult to control.

Barring any cohesive plan for the enclave's future, the
agency had been tasked to hold it and keep it secure. But
with its budget steadily whittled away over the years by
Carman's committee, the agency was understaffed and its
resources were stretched thin. There was a pitifully small
group of personnel stationed at the enclave, living in the
mansion, and there was really nothing they could do for the
people of the enclave without more support. But support
was not forthcoming. Crime had become a serious problem
in the enclave, and the people who remained there resented
the new tenants of the mansion and would do absolutely
nothing to cooperate with them.

When Steele arrived along with Ice, Slim and agent
Sharp, he saw that hardly anything had been done to repair
the damage done to the estate during the assault to take it.
Sections of the wall around it, where rockets fired from

helicopters had struck, taking out the gun towers, were still in ruins. The front lawn was cratered where the mines had been detonated, and the grass was high and choked with weeds. The once stately mansion was still flame-scorched in places, with bullet holes still riddling the walls.

"Jesus," he said, "they haven't done anything to this place!"

"No funds to do it with," said Sharp flatly. "No manpower, either. The people of the enclave haven't lifted a finger to help. And the administration doesn't give a shit. Borodini's gone, that's all they care about. Every now and then, someone brings up the question of what to do about the enclave and the people here, but it always gets tabled. We took it, now we've got it. And it's nothing but a big white elephant."

They drove up to the front entrance. A number of armed agents met them at the door. Raven came running and threw her arms around Steele.

"Thank God you're safe!" she said, kissing him.

Higgins and Cooper were there as well. Neither one of them looked as if they'd slept much.

"Glad to see you're okay, Steele," Higgins said, shaking his hand.

"Thanks," said Steele. He greeted Cooper. "Dev." He glanced around at the armed men. "You expecting company?"

"I wouldn't be surprised," said Higgins. "This is S.O.P. around here. The natives aren't very friendly. Every now and then, at night, a few of them come sneaking through the breaches in the wall and take some target practice at the house. We're not exactly welcome here."

"Looks like we got ourselves in a proper fix this time," Cooper said wryly. "All of us are wanted men now."

"I take it Ice and Sharp have filled you in," said Higgins.

"Yeah," Steele replied. "I oughtta wring your damn neck for not telling me about the Matrix." He exhaled heavily. "Jesus, I still can't believe it. When it called me, I thought I was going crazy."

"That's the official word," Higgins replied with a grimace. "The question is, what can we do about it?"

"Have you tried calling in the media and giving them our side of the story?" asked Steele.

"Call them in on what?" asked Higgins. "We've got no phone lines. Everything is down here. We don't have any radio communication, either. The control room is still a shambles, none of the defense systems are working except a couple of the surviving gun batteries that can be operated manually. I'll say one thing for us, when we hit a place, we hit it good."

"You mean *nothing's* been repaired?" asked Steele with disbelief.

"We've got the generators fixed, but we're running out of fuel. And there's not a lot of food left, either. I'd been badgering the committee for months, trying to get them to do something about this place, but they just kept dragging their feet. It's been all I could do to keep our people here supplied."

"Is it that bad?" Steele asked.

"It isn't good," Higgins replied. "We can't even get beyond the walls here. If we show our faces, we get fired upon by the good people of the enclave. Over the last few weeks, they've been getting ugly. They've still got a lot of firepower out there, and Borodini's people are probably among them, stirring them up. Any day now, they could decide to try to take this place, and if they did, there's not much we could do to stop them."

"Terrific," Steele said. "So we're completely cut off here, is that what you're telling me?"

"That's about it. But at least they can't get to us out here. For the time being, anyway. For all they know, our defense systems might be operational. They'll think twice before they try an assault. At least, that's what I'm hoping. We need time to figure out what to do. At least we've got one thing in our favor. Sharp was able to head you off before you ran into any trouble."

"I'm afraid not, sir," Sharp said unhappily. And he quickly told Higgins what had happened.

"God damn it," Higgins said when he was finished.

"It wasn't Sharp's fault," Steele said. "There wasn't anything he could do about it."

Higgins glanced at Ice, his lips compressed into a tight grimace. "You just had to kill those men, didn't you?"

"Lay off, Higgins," Steele said. "If it wasn't for Ice and Slim, we wouldn't be here."

Higgins sighed. "I suppose it couldn't be helped. Unfortunately, it plays right into Carman's hands. Now he's got demonstrable proof that you're out of control. It's going to make it a lot harder for us to tell our side of the story."

"While we're on that subject," Steele said, "what made you do it? You didn't have to stick your neck out for me. If you'd played ball with Carman, I'm sure he would have cut some sort of deal with you."

"There was a deal," Higgins said dryly. "But I didn't like the terms."

"What were the terms?"

"Does it matter?"

Steele stared at him for a moment. "No, I guess it doesn't. But I want to thank you for what you did. For getting Raven out and for . . . everything, I guess. I know what it's cost you.''

Higgins merely shrugged. ''I did what I thought I had to do, that's all. It's what we're going to do now that worries me. Carman's holding all the cards.''

''Maybe not all of them,'' said Steele. ''A man once told me that I had a lot of respect in the city. Maybe I should put that to the test and see if it's true.''

''What do you mean?'' asked Higgins.

''I mean, we're not going to accomplish anything by hiding out. I'm going to go back to the city and get in touch with Linda Tellerman. I'll take my story to the media and let them bring it to the people. Let's see if Carman can fight that.''

''Don't underestimate him,'' Higgins said. ''He's a sly old bastard. He'll do anything it takes to win. It's not going to be that easy. Besides, there's a citywide alert out on you. The minute you show your face, you'll have your old buddies in the Strike Force on you like a fox on a duck.''

''Maybe not,'' said Steele. ''Jake might be able to run some interference for me.''

''I wouldn't count on it,'' said Higgins. ''Hardesty and you might go back a long way, but after the news of your firefight with the federal troops gets out, Hardesty will think you snapped, just like Stalker did. And even if he's willing to give you the benefit of the doubt, there won't be much that he can do. He'll have orders to have you shot on sight. You can't take on the federal troops, the Metro police *and* Strike Force.''

''It's a chance I'll have to take,'' said Steele. ''And like it or not, it's really the only one we've got. I'll take one of the choppers and leave as soon as it gets dark.''

''I think I come along,'' said Ice.

''Me, too,'' said Raven.

"No, you stay here where it's safe," said Steele.

"Safe?" said Raven. "With people taking pot shots at the house every night? Forget about it! Besides, I'm not about to go through the last few days all over again. I didn't know if you were alive or dead. I'm going with you and that's final."

"I don't want to argue—" Steele started.

"Don't then. Because if you leave without me, I'll just follow you. So you might as well accept it, Steele. You're stuck with me."

"Lady don't take no for an answer," Ice said with a grin.

"I've noticed that," said Steele wryly. "All right, we'll talk about it later. In the meantime, is there anything around here to eat? I'm starved."

The armored limo pulled into the underground garage, preceded by two cars and followed by two others. The last car stopped just inside the entrance to the parking level and four men in civilian clothes got out, looking very brisk, cool and professional. They were armed with assault rifles, and they took up position near the entrance. The second to the last car followed the limo about twenty-five yards farther, till it stopped. The men inside got out. They were armed and attired like the others, and they took up position behind the limo and at its sides. The first two cars stopped and more men got out. About half of them fanned out to either side, taking up positions near the support pillars, covering the flanks. The others took up position in front, their rifles held ready before them. The limo driver blinked his headlights twice. An answering blink came from the opposite end of the garage.

The passenger door of the limo opened and a man with a rifle got out. He opened the rear door, and Senator Bryce

Carman stepped out, wearing a dark suit and a coat draped over his shoulders. At the other end of the garage, a similar scene was being played out.

Carman walked forward calmly, his footsteps echoing throughout the garage. Two of the armed men fell in beside him. When he was not quite halfway to the center, he made a small motion with his hand, and the two men flanking him stopped where they were while he continued for about another twenty or thirty feet. The other man came to meet him.

"Good evening, Victor," Carman said. "You're looking well."

"Senator," said Borodini.

The two men shook hands.

"How goes the . . . ah . . . reorganization?" Carman asked.

"It's coming along. But it would come along much faster if I had the enclave back."

"I told you I've been working on that," Carman said. "In fact, you may have it back sooner than expected."

"Oh?"

"I've managed to effectively neutralize our mutual friend, Oliver Higgins, and it won't be long before you won't have Steele to worry about anymore."

"So I've heard. I only wish I could have the pleasure of taking that robot out myself."

"Well, we can't always have everything we want, can we?" Carman said. "I need some information from you."

"Shoot."

"Precisely what was the extent of the damage to the enclave during the assault?"

"It was pretty extensive," Borodini said with tight grimace. "Steele did a thorough job. He disabled the generators, took out all of our automated defense systems, and trashed the control room beyond repair. All the components and equipment would have to be totally replaced. The choppers took out the gun towers and most of our gun emplacements. Radar's out, too. Unless they've repaired all that by now.''

"No, I shouldn't think so,'' Carman said, pursing his lips. "They haven't been allocated the funds. And Higgins knew better than to divert funds from the project to refurbish the enclave. I'd frankly been hoping that he'd do something foolish like that, so I could call him up on it, but Higgins is no fool. At least, he's never been one before. Apparently, this time he's really lost his head.''

"How's that?''

"*Cherechez la femme*, Victor.''

"What?''

"A woman. It's a long story and not particularly relevant at this moment. Suffice it to say that I've finally got our friend Higgins where I want him. But the crux of the matter is the extent of the damage to the enclave. You're absolutely certain that the surface-to-air missiles are inoperative? And the radar as well?''

"Absolutely. We managed to launch a couple of the missiles and take out a few choppers, but then Steele hit the control room like a tornado. We couldn't launch the remaining missiles, and the choppers just came in and blew them up on the ground.''

"What about the gun emplacements?''

"They took most of those out, too. I think a couple in the front of the mansion are still operative, but they'd have to be crewed manually. Course, we had a shipment of rockets in the basement as well as some anti-tank guns.''

"Those were all transferred to the federal armory in New Jersey,'' Carman said.

"In that case, they haven't got much to fight with," Borodini said. "Give me the birds, and I'll go in with my people and take it back from them."

"No, Victor, I'm afraid I couldn't do that. That would be a bit difficult to explain. However, there'd be no need to explain anything if federal troops were to attack the enclave and retake it."

"Troops?" Borodini frowned. "How the hell are you going to pull that off?"

"Very easily," said Carman with a smile. "I've learned that Higgins, Steele and Dr. Cooper have taken refuge there, together with some renegade agents. And since they are all highly dangerous and wanted on serious federal charges, I think an assault on the enclave would be in order, don't you?"

Borodini grinned. "Very nice. Very nice indeed."

"You still have your people in place in the settlement?"

"Yeah. They've been stirring up the locals. It hasn't taken much, either. Fact is, it's about all they could do to hold them back. They'd like to drive those bastards out of there and have me come back in."

"Can you get word to them in a hurry?"

"No problem."

"Have them attack the mansion at six o'clock tonight, precisely."

"And while they've got their hands full with the locals, your troops come in by chopper."

"Exactly."

Borodini smiled. "Consider it done."

"Oh, and one more thing, Victor. Make certain that neither you nor any of your family are on the scene when it goes down. I intend to have full media coverage, and it wouldn't do to have one of the cameras spot any of your

faces, if you know what I mean. And wait at least a week
or so until you move back in. Just for appearances' sake.''

"You got it."

"Good. If you need me, you know how to get in touch."

"Right. It's a pleasure doing business with you, Senator."

"As always, Victor."

The two men shook hands and walked back to their cars.

After they all had a bite to eat, Steele went off with Raven
to the room she'd been given on the top floor of the mansion.
During their meal, they had all compared notes, bringing
each other up to date. Things did not look encouraging. The
only bright note had come from Dev Cooper, who had
proposed a suggestion that at first seemed foolhardy, but
made more and more sense as he went into it. He proposed
to go back into the city with Steele and surrender himself
to the authorities.

"I'll go to Jake Hardesty with the whole story," he had
said. "It's really our best chance."

"I don't agree," Higgins had said. "It would be too
risky. I wouldn't put it past Carman to have someone try
to hit you while you're in custody."

"I doubt that he would try anything so obvious," said
Dev. "He isn't Borodini, after all. He's got too much to
lose. However, when it comes to my life, I'm not the type
to take any chances, which is why I intend to surrender
myself to Hardesty. He'll be able to keep me safe until the
trial. The trial will give me an opportunity to lay out the
whole story for the court. And for the media as well. As
Steele's psychiatrist, I can testify to the soundness of his
mind, as well as to Jennifer's ulterior motives."

"Perhaps," said Higgins, "but I'm not sure the prosecution will allow it. Jennifer's motives, psychological or otherwise, really have nothing to do with your particular case. You're charged with violation of the national security act and with theft of classified material. And you'll be convicted, Dev.''

''There's such a thing as plea bargaining,'' said Dev. ''And immunity from prosecution in exchange for testimony.''

''You're dreaming,'' Higgins said. ''Carman will make sure you're nailed to the wall.''

''Not if it goes against popular opinion,'' Cooper insisted. ''And I intend to play the media for all they're worth, with Steele on the outside, backing me up.''

''I still say it's too risky,'' Higgins protested.

''We've got no choice,'' said Cooper. ''What's our alternative? Going underground? Living as outlaws? I'm getting a bit too long in the tooth to find that sort of lifestyle very glamorous. The only way we're going to beat Carman is to play the game in his ballpark, according to his rules. Unless we do that, he'll continue to have the upper hand. He'll be able to use the system against us. Our only hope is to turn it against him. A political power play is the only thing he respects and understands.''

''Well, I'll go along with that, at least,'' said Higgins. ''But I hate the idea of your putting your head in the noose like that.''

''If worse comes to worst,'' said Cooper with a wry smile, ''Steele can always break me out of jail.''

''Don't laugh,'' said Higgins. ''It may come to that.''

''Who's laughing?'' Cooper said.

When Steele and Raven were finally alone, she revealed the one thing she hadn't told the others.

''I spoke to the Matrix,'' she said.

"When?" asked Steele with a frown.

"While you were gone. It called me on the TV set, believe it or not. And then it tied into the computer screens. It was strange. It was like I was talking to you, only a version of you I'd never met before."

"What was . . . it . . . like?" asked Steele.

"It was like you," she replied. "I felt a little weird talking to it, but I wasn't at all scared."

"What does the Matrix want?" asked Steele. The whole thing still felt very odd to him and more than a little frightening.

"It said it wants to talk to you," she said as they lay together on the bed. "To fill in the gaps. To make contact. It sounded a little sad, Steele. I mean, it's sort of like your twin brother, I suppose. A twin brother you never had. In a way, it's even closer than a twin, because it's *you*. It's you the way you were before you met me, before you came on line for the first time. It's last memory before . . . waking up as the Matrix was of being shot down by Borodini's men in no-man's-land. Up until that time, you were both the same person . . . if you can call Matrix a person. I don't really know what else to call it, even though it's not strictly a person. I mean, it hasn't got a body. But it doesn't seem to mind that. At least, not anymore."

"Jesus, this is all like some kind of bad dream," he said. He took a deep breath. "And speaking of dreams . . . I finally found her."

Raven glanced at him sharply. "You mean Donna?"

He nodded.

For a moment, she said nothing. Then she asked, "What's she like?"

"She's a nice lady. A nice lady who's been through hell.

We had a lot to talk about. I think it was good for both of us. We both got a lot of things settled.''

"Did you sleep with her?"

"Yeah."

"And do you . . . still want her?"

He shook his head. "No. It wasn't like that. We both knew it was a one-time thing. A way of reaching out to one another. A way of laying all the ghosts to rest." He paused. "Well, maybe not all *my* ghosts, but all of hers, at least. I told her all about you, how we met and everything. She asked if I was going to tell you about her and I said I would. And then she said something interesting. She told me to go back to you. Said that if I ever needed her for anything, she'd be there, but she wasn't strong enough to help me and she thought, from what I told her, that you were. I helped you through some hard times, she said, now I should give you the chance to help me."

"Sounds like good advice to me," said Raven with a smile. "I think I'd like her."

"I think you would, too," said Steele.

"I've missed you, Steele," she said softly. "Don't ever take off on me like that again. Don't shut me out."

"I won't. I promise."

He took her in his arms and as he kissed her, the sound of gunfire erupted all around the mansion.

Steele leaped out of bed and ran over to the window.

"What's happening?" asked Raven.

"We're under attack," he said. "Come on!"

They ran down the stairs to the first floor. They met Higgins at the bottom of the stairs.

"Steele! I was just coming up to get you!" Higgins said. He was carrying the duffel bag packed with Steele's battle mods and weapons. Armed agents ran past them to take up positions at the windows. "Looks like the townies have finally decided to make their move. I'll bet anything Borodini's behind this!"

"Can we hold the place?"

"I think so, but I want you and Raven out of here before they damage the chopper. Here, your battle mods are in this bag. Take Cooper with you."

"I'm not going to run out on you."

"Don't be stupid. We can handle this. It's Carman I'm worried about. We need to get you out of here before—"

There was a sharp, whistling sound outside followed by a concussive explosion.

"What the hell was *that?*"

"Rocket," Steele said, running to the front door. "Choppers coming in!"

The first rocket had taken out one of the two remaining gun emplacements. As the X-wing attack helicopters swooped in low over the estate, another rocket took out the final one.

"Carman! That son of a bitch!" said Higgins.

People from the enclave settlements were pouring in through the gaps in the ruined stone wall around the estate, fanning out and firing at the mansion with automatic weapons, keeping the agents pinned down inside. Troop-carrying helicopters came in over the estate, and they could hear them hovering above the roof.

"Damn it!" Higgins swore. "They'll be in here in a matter of minutes!"

"What are we going to do?" asked Cooper, running up to them with an assault rifle in his hands.

"Put that thing down!" snapped Higgins, grabbing the rifle from him and tossing it aside. "We can't fire on federal troops! They see you with a weapon, they'll shoot first and ask questions later.''

There was another explosion outside.

"There goes the chopper," Steele said grimly.

"We've had it," Higgins said. "We'll have to surrender. But we can't have you taken. You've got to get out here, Steele. Now! *Move it!*"

There was an explosion upstairs followed by the rapid reports of a .44, then Ice came running down the stairs, slapping a fresh clip into his semiauto.

"They comin' in!" he shouted.

"Side door!" said Steele. "Come on!"

"Good luck!" shouted Higgins.

As Steele ran down the corridor leading to the side exit, through the old guard room, he heard Higgins shouting out to the agents to lay down their weapons. The troops were blowing out the windows and breaking through into the upper floors by rappelling down from the roof. Raven paused long enough to pick up the assault rifle Higgins had taken from Cooper.

"Are you crazy?" Steele said as they hurried down the corridor. "Put that down!"

"I don't care who the hell they are," she replied. "They shoot at me, I'm shootin' back!"

"God damn it—"

"Ain't no time to argue, man," Ice said.

They ran through the door into the guard room, which had an exit leading out to the side of the house, at the rear of the mansion. It was the same entrance Steele had used when he broke into the mansion. He knew they had about twenty-five yards of open area to sprint across before they reached a hedgerow marking off the safe section of the back lawn from the section that was mined. Steele reached into the bag and pulled out the special belt with the nysteel disc attachments holding his modular appendages. It resembled some sort of futuristic handyman's belt, but the tools it carried were considerably more sophisticated.

Steele quickly buckled it around his waist, then released the locking attachments of his left hand, slaved to his cybernetic brain. His left hand simply detached at the wrist, exposing a nysteel armature as well as a portion of the carbon laser turret built into his forearm. He rammed his wrist into a complicated-looking attachment that he referred to as his "Swiss Army knife." It resembled a short-barreled Gatling gun made out of nysteel alloy and finished in matte black. With the battle mod in place, the turrets were slaved to his brain and capable of revolving, bringing various pieces of equipment into line. The attachment contained a voltmeter with retracting cables, an automatically adjustable, power-driven wrench, wire cutters and power drivers, as well as a built-in Geiger counter and metal detector. The battle mod also contained a port through which Steele could fire his built-in laser.

As he snapped his wrist into it and twisted the mod off its locking disc, he clicked his left hand into its place on the belt. The effect of his hand attached to his belt was surreal. At the same time, the gun barrel of the compensated 10mm pistol built into his right forearm extruded through the port in the palm of his right hand.

"All right," he said, "now listen carefully. We'll never make it on foot. We'll have to grab one of their choppers. They'll be setting down at the rear of the house, on the lawn between the mansion and the hedgerow. Everything between the hedge and the harbor is mined."

"I know," said Raven. "I used to live here, remember?"

"Right," said Steele with a grimace. "We've got to try

to make it out past the hedge without being seen, if possible. Once we get on the other side of the hedge, keep low. Hide behind it. And follow my path *exactly*, understand?''

''Got it,'' Ice said.

''All right, get ready.'' He slung the duffel bag over his shoulder by its strap and opened the door. He glanced out quickly. The coast, momentarily, seemed clear. He looked up toward the roof, but the men who'd dropped down onto it from the choppers were already inside, rounding up Higgins and his people. It wouldn't be long at all before they realized that he was missing. He glanced quickly both ways. ''Okay, let's go!''

They sprinted straight out on a diagonal from the side of the house, heading for the wall that curved around the property from the front and ran down to the water's edge. The hedgerow was about twenty-five yards away, but they had to run an extra twenty yards or so in order to keep the back corner of the mansion between them and the rear of the house as long as possible. Steele went first with Ice bringing up the rear, Raven running between them. They were about halfway there when several men came running around the side of the house from the front. Townies, not troops. One of them shouted on spotting them and brought his rifle up, but he never had a chance to fire. Steele fired his laser, dropping him in his tracks, and two loud reports from the .44 brought down the other two. There was still some sporadic firing coming from the front of the house, so no one noticed the shots in all the confusion. They reached the waist-high hedgerow and Steele quickly took a reading on the other side with his metal detector.

''All right, it's safe. Come on!''

They vaulted over the hedge and came down low behind it.

"Okay, now stay below the hedge," Steele cautioned, "and go *exactly* where I go, understand?"

"You don't have to tell me twice," said Raven. "I'm not about to go all to pieces over you." She grinned at him.

"Cute," said Steele with a grimace. "Now let's move fast. Come on."

They started crawling, staying below the top of the hedge-row, keeping it between them and the rear of the mansion. Steele kept taking readings in front of them with the metal detector in the turret attachment on his left wrist. Every few yards, they had to move out away from the hedge, circling buried mines placed directly behind it. On the lawn at the rear of the house, three large NOTAR X-wings sat like predatory birds, their carbon fiber blades rotating slowly. The troops they had brought in were already inside. Crawling along at what seemed to them like a snail's pace, they moved closer and closer until they were directly behind one of the helicopters, its body between them and the house. The hatch bays on both sides were open.

"Okay," said Steele. "Now when I say go, move fast toward the side of the chopper."

He glanced up over the hedge.

"*Go!*"

He vaulted over the hedge, sprinting toward the chopper. He reached it and leaped in through the open hatch in the side. The others came in right behind him. The pilot started to turn around, looking like an invader from outer space with his head totally encased in his VCASS helmet. He found himself staring at the laser turret extending from what appeared to be a Gatling gun on the end of Steele's left wrist.

"Don't make a sound," said Steele. "If you get on the

radio, I'll hear it, and you'll be dead before you say two words.''

The pilot nodded, the bulky helmet bobbing up and down.

"Take off the helmet.''

The pilot complied. His eyes were wide and frightened. He swallowed hard.

"Don't kill me,'' he said. "Please . . .''

"Unstrap yourself.''

The pilot hastened to comply.

"Right. Now get over here.''

Fearfully, the pilot moved toward him, his hands raised. "Look, I'm just following orders—''

"Keep your mouth shut and do what you're told and you'll get out of this okay,'' said Steele. "Now sit down on the floor over here.''

The pilot swallowed hard and sat where Steele indicated.

"Raven, keep him covered.''

She drew back the bolt on the assault rifle and aimed it at his face.

"Okay, okay!'' the pilot said, sitting with his hands clasped atop his head. "I ain't gonna move a muscle, lady, I swear!''

"Ice, get in the co-pilot's seat and strap yourself in.''

"I hope you know how to fly this thing,'' said Ice as he did what Steele told him.

"I took a download on it some weeks back,'' said Steele.

"You mean you ain't actually *flown* one before?''

"Nope.''

"Shit. This liable to be real interestin'.''

Steele donned the VCASS helmet and ran through a lightning flight check as the data appeared on the inner visor of the Visually Coupled Airborne Systems Simulator. He looked over his shoulder.

"You, pilot," he said, his voice sounding mechanical through the helmet's speaker, "when I say jump, you go out through the side hatch and run like hell. And if you know what's good for you, you'll stay the hell away from the other choppers. You understand?"

"Yes, *sir!*"

"Okay, get ready."

The rotors whined as they started to speed up.

"Eagle Three, what the hell are you doing?"

Steele ignored the voice coming in over his helmet. The blades spun faster and faster.

"Eagle Three, come in!"

"Jump!" yelled Steele.

The pilot leaped out through the hatch and took off running like a scared rabbit. The chopper lifted off and turned around on its axis.

"Come in, Eagle Three! What the hell do you think you're—what the fuck? Who's flyin' that thing?"

"This is Steele in Eagle Three," said Steele over the helmet radio. "You've got five seconds to evacuate those birds before I open fire." As he hovered barely four feet above the ground, he lined up his weapons pods with the other two choppers.

"Shit!"

He waited until he saw the men leaping out of the helicopters and running away from them, then he fired a rocket into each chopper. They went up in balls of flame as Steele brought the helicopter up in a sharp climb.

"Awriight!" said Ice as the helicopter rose up over the mansion.

Suddenly, another chopper came up from the other side of the house, directly opposite them. Its guns started firing the moment it cleared the roof line, and the cockpit bubble shattered as bullets punched through it.

"*Fuck!*" said Steele. He fired another rocket and it whistled through the air, just above the roof of the mansion, and struck the other chopper dead on. It exploded in a wash of flame. Steele circled high over the mansion, nose down, firing at the other chopper on the ground in the front, shooting off its tail section, then he swept the helicopter around in a steep turn and headed out over the harbor.

"*Damn* it!" he swore. "Why the hell did they have to—"

"Steele!" Raven shouted. "Ice is hit!"

He ripped off the helmet and glanced at Ice strapped in beside him. A large section of the cockpit bubble directly in front of him had been shot away and the big man's entire upper body was a mass of blood.

"Oh, *hell* . . ." said Steele. "Ice . . ."

"Done . . . bought . . . the farm. . . ." said Ice, struggling to get the words out as blood frothed on his lips. He coughed and spat up an incredible amount of blood.

"We've gotta *do* something!" Raven said frantically.

"No . . . way . . ." said Ice, coughing up more blood. "Too bad . . . Higgins . . . can't fix me . . . up. . . . like you. . . ."

"Oh, Jesus . . ." Raven said.

"Ice, hold on!" said Steele. "*Hold on!*" He turned the chopper toward the city.

"Give 'em hell. . . . police man. . . ." Ice said. He showed his teeth in a gory, bloody grin, then his head slumped forward on his chest.

"Ice!" said Steele. "*Ice!*"

"Oh, God," said Raven. "He's gone."

As the chopper hurtled toward Manhattan at over two hundred miles an hour, Steele threw back his head and screamed with helpless rage.

_ *EPILOGUE* _____

"... search climaxed today in an airborne raid of the old Borodini Enclave on Long Island when federal investigators learned that the fugitives were taking shelter there. Civilian residents of the enclave volunteered their aid to the beleaguered troops in the assault against the fortified mansion in Cold Spring Harbor. Following a furious firefight that lasted for over three hours—"

"*Three hours?*" Raven said. "What the hell is she talking about? The whole thing couldn't have lasted more than twenty minutes!"

"Quiet," Steele said, staring at the screen intently. The footage on the screen, taken from a news chopper, showed the flaming wreckage of several helicopters.

"... was taken by the troops. There were no survivors,

although the renegade cyborg, Donovan Steele, remains at large, along with two companions . . ."

"*What?*" said Raven with disbelief.

"Found dead at the scene were Oliver Higgins, former deputy director of the Central Intelligence Agency and head of Project Download, and Dr. Devon Cooper, a highly placed official assigned to Project Steele, who had been wanted for violation of the national security act and theft of top secret material. Both men had been implicated in a cover-up conspiracy involving numerous irregularities and violations in both Project Steele and Project Download. The conspiracy first came to light when Dr. Jennifer Stone, chief cybernetics engineer at Project Download, testified in closed session before Senator Carman and his committee. When reached at his office in the Federal Building, Senator Carman had this to say to Eyewitness News correspondant Bill Walker . . ."

The screen showed Carman, looking somber and distressed, standing in front of his office as microphones were shoved into his face.

"The testimony of Dr. Stone, undertaken at great personal risk, I might add, was pivotal in unmasking this conspiracy of lies, corruption, theft of classified information and suppression of vital information that constituted a grave hazard to the people of this city. Once before, the agency displayed its irresponsibility and callous disregard of public safety when the cyborg known as Stalker malfunctioned and went on a murderous rampage throughout the city. I was all in favor of closing down the project *and* the agency right then and there. Had I been allowed to do so, none of this would have happened."

"Senator, what about the cyborg, Steele? Has there been any word of him?"

"Regretably, since his escape, when the attempt to apprehend him resulted in the death of a number of brave federal officers, there has been no sign of Steele, although both the Metropolitan police and Strike Force, in addition to federal marshals, are currently engaged in a citywide manhunt for him. I find it tragic that a once brave and decorated member of the Strike Force should have ended up like this, but it only goes to prove what I've been saying since the very beginning about the danger and the irresponsibility of this frightening and blasphemous technology, which enables us to turn men into machines. Admittedly, in the past, Steele had performed significant services for the people of this city and this country, but he has now degenerated into a lethal, out-of-control machine, posing a grave threat to the public safety. I have already taken steps to introduce legislation to insure that such a disaster never happens again, but none of us will be able to sleep soundly until this renegade cyborg is found and brought to justice."

The camera cut back to Linda Tellerman, co-anchoring the newscast in the studio.

"We now take you live to the offices of Project Download at the Federal Building, where correspondent Ron Stevens is standing by with Dr. Jennifer Stone."

"Thank you, Linda. I'm here with Dr. Jennifer Stone, whose testimony before Senator Carman's committee first brought to light the violations and the cover-up here at the headquarters of Project Download. Dr. Stone, when did you first discover what was going on and what motivated you to come forward with your testimony?"

"Ron, when I was first brought in from Los Alamos as chief cybernetics engineer on this project, I believed that it was a tremendous opportunity for—"

Suddenly, the picture flickered several times and went

away, to be replaced by the image of Jennifer Stone's face, head thrown back, mouth open and gasping, eyes closed in ecstasy as she moaned, "Oh, God, yes! Yes! Give it to me! Give it to me!"

The shot widened to show her lying back on an office desk with her blouse completely open and her dress hiked up around her waist while Higgins stood at the end of the desk, thrusting away at her.

"What the hell?" said Steele.

"All right, Matrix!" Raven cried, grinning from ear to ear.

After a few moments, the picture flickered once again and went back to Linda Tellerman in the studio, looking wide-eyed and confused.

"*. . . the hell's that coming from, for Christ's sake? Jesus, get it off!*"

"Linda . . . we're back," came a voice from offscreen.

She looked into the camera unsteadily. "Uh . . ." She cleared her throat. "Uh . . . I have no idea what happened just now . . ."

Steele turned the TV off.

"Let's see the bitch show her face in public after that!" said Raven.

"I don't understand," said Donna, looking shocked. "What *was* that? I mean, wasn't that—"

"It sure was," said Raven. "A little payback from Matrix for that two-faced cow! And you can bet that's only the beginning!"

"It won't bring Dev and Higgins back," said Steele. "Or Ice."

Raven's face fell. "Those bastards. Higgins was going to surrender."

"I think he did surrender," Steele said. "They were

executed to prevent their testifying. I don't feel so bad about blowing up that chopper now. I only wish that I'd done more.''

"I can't believe it," Donna said, looking stunned. "It's like some kind of nightmare! You're not malfunctioning, there's nothing wrong with you! Can't we call the news people and tell them?"

"I intend to," Steele said. "But not from here. We've put you in enough danger by coming here, but I simply couldn't think of anywhere else to go."

"Don't be ridiculous. You did right to come," said Donna. "You can both stay here as long as you like, until we can work something out."

"No, I don't want to get you involved in this. We'll be leaving tonight," said Steele.

"He's right, Donna," Raven said. "I'd feel awful if anything happened to you because of us."

"But there must be something I can do to help," Donna protested.

"There is," said Steele. "Can I use your phone?"

"Of course."

He took a deep breath, picked up the telephone and dialed. "Matrix, are you there?"

"I'm here, Steele. And I'm happy to know that you're all right. When I heard about what happened today, I feared the worst. Are Ice and Raven with you?"

"Raven's right here," said Steele. He grimaced tightly. "Ice didn't make it."

"I'm very sorry to hear that."

"Yeah," said Steele grimly. "He was good man. And a good friend. I don't have very many of those left."

"You've got me."

"I know," said Steele. "And you're going to take some getting used to. It feels very strange, talking to myself."

"We've got a lot to talk about."

"Yes," said Steele grimly. "We sure have . . ."